PRISCILLA THE GREAT TOO LITTLE, TOO LATE

PRISCILLA THE GREAT TOO LITTLE, TOO LATE

SYBIL NELSON

LITTLE PRINCE PUBLISHING

Published by Little Prince Publishing in Charleston, South Carolina.
Cover Design: Glendon Haddix
.

ISBN-13: **978-1466222267** (CreateSpace)
ISBN-10: **1466222263**

Printed in the United States of America
Visit www.LittlePrincePublishing.com

To
Fatima,
Thanks for
reading.

Sybil Nelson

Chapter1:
Marco's Metal Fist

Marco's left fist connected with my right eye. I saw stars. Literally, I saw stars. And they weren't the kinds of stars I saw a couple of hours ago the last time Marco touched me. That time, he had his lips on mine and I saw the kind of stars that made you ridiculously happy and make all your girlfriends crazy jealous. The kind of stars that say, "That's right, I'm frenching a hot French boy." Nope, definitely not those kinds of stars. These were the "Oh snap! I'm gonna get killed by a human robot" kind of stars.

I did a backflip out of the way trying to buy some time before I would actually have to fight him back. I didn't want to hurt him. I knew he wouldn't try to kill me on purpose. This was all because of Colonel Selliwood. The real Marco cared about me and would do anything for me. He'd told me that himself. I didn't want to do any permanent damage to him. But if he kept bashing my face in I'd have no choice.

I stole a glance at Tai pounding away at the computer, trying to figure out how to undo whatever had been done to Marco.

"How's it going over there, Tai?" I asked, faking calmness as I dodged a roundhouse kick from the super-powered metal maniac who used to be my super-powered crush.

"I'm doing the best I can," she said in a shaky voice. I sure hoped she didn't start crying. That was so not what we needed right now. I knew Tai could handle this. She had to. After all, what was the point of having a genius best friend if she couldn't hack into a few computers and undo a little mind control programming from evil villains?

"I don't know how long I can hold him off, Tai. He's —" I didn't get to finish my thought as Marco landed a right hook to the side of my face. My mouth filled with the metallic taste of blood. This was not usually how I tasted metal when I was around Marco.

I spat a mouthful of blood on the floor. Yes, I spat. I knew that was gross but swallowing a mouthful of blood is grosser (is that a word?).

Oh, I was so tired of bleeding. I'd been kicked, punched, and shot. And that was just tonight! That was it. He was going down. I didn't care how cute or how good of a kisser he was. I reared back and landed a punch to his gut.

"OW!" I cried out in pain. Tears instantly welled up in my eyes. "Holy hot chocolate! That hurt!" Marco in metal form was indestructible. I might've just broken my hand on his stomach.

I looked into his cold blank eyes. He gave no reaction to my pain. If I was fighting Xi, she would at least laugh at me. This was like fighting an emotionless robot. It was kind of scary.

"You okay, Priss?" Tai called over to me.

I threw a blast of fire with my fingers into Robot Marco's face to give myself a second to get away. Now it was his turn to scream in pain. Huh? So even in metal form he could still feel the heat. I'd have to use that.

"I'm fine," I yelled to Tai after I hid behind a lab table. Well, that was a lie. I totally was *not* fine. I stared at the bent and bloody fingers of my left hand. So much for that manicure.

Marco's metal feet clanged against the tiles of the huge laboratory we were in. Whatever Colonel Selliwood had done to him, it obviously affected his common sense. He should've found me ten seconds ago since there wasn't much to hide behind in here. There was a glass pentagon-shaped cubicle in the center of the room where Tai worked on the computer. He should have been able to look straight through it and see me but instead he was still turning around in circles with a determinedly blank, yet slightly confused, expression on

4

his face. His confusion might be my only hope. Fighting him hand-to-hand would be plain stupid, unless I was ready to break every bone in my body.

Leaping out from my hiding place, I jumped on a table and started blasting him with my fire power. His screams of pain brought tears to my eyes. I didn't want to hurt him but I had no choice. He marched blindly toward the source of the fire so I flipped out of the way and started blasting him from another angle. He fell to one knee still crying out in agony. I thought I had him beat so I stopped shooting. A second later, however, he disappeared. He'd used his super speed to get away. Now it was my turn to spin around in confused circles. Where did he go? Well, that question was painfully answered as soon as I felt his metal fingers around my neck.

I gasped as I tried to scratch, hit, and kick my way free. Nothing worked. He was squeezing the life out of me. I started blasting his face with fire, but I had so little oxygen in my lungs I didn't have the energy. The stream was weak and started to fade.

I saw spots. The room dimmed to black. My life started flashing before me. Don't laugh, it did.

I saw myself at six years old pouring milk in Kyle's hair because a commercial said "It does a body good" and I thought his body could use some good.

I saw myself in third grade, a.k.a. "The Era of Unfortunate Hair," meeting Tai for the first time right after I punched Kyle in the stomach for picking on said unfortunate hair.

I saw myself standing on my front porch last November after escaping the Selliwood Institute when Kyle asked me to the River Day dance.

Then I saw myself on our farm in Missouri having my first kiss on my thirteenth birthday. Once again, it had been with Kyle.

Why was it that all my memories involved Kyle? I mean, I was a genetically-enhanced superhero who defeated evil villains every time I turned around, yet all I could think of was my first boyfriend while I was being choked to death by my second boyfriend.

For some reason, thinking about Kyle gave me a boost of energy. I really wanted to see him again one day even though he currently hated my guts because of, well, Marco. I focused that energy into my fingers and sent flames into both of Marco's ears. He released my neck and clutched the sides of his head.

I ran away and hid again while gasping for air and rubbing my sore neck.

"Uh, Priss, we got company," Tai said.

"What do you mean?" My voice was barely a whisper so she probably didn't hear me. Thankfully, she continued.

"It's Ian. He's coming this way and, uh, I don't think he likes us very much anymore."

"What's your point? He's never liked us!"

"Uh, my point is he looks about as deadly as Marco right now. And he's leading the others right to us!"

I shook my head in disbelief. There was no way I could defeat all of them by myself. How did I get into this? More importantly, how the heck was I gonna get out of it?

7

Chapter 2:
Marco's Metal Embrace

This episode of the tragic comedy called my life started two weeks ago, right after my mother tried to kill my father. Yeah, that's right. Kill. She had stabbed him in the chest in the middle of the night right before leaping out of the window and disappearing into darkness. After that, my brothers, father and I had gathered and hid in the storm shelter.

That was how we ended up trapped and fearing for our lives.

Someone was banging on the door trying to get in. My brother Josh steadied a rifle, ready to shoot whoever entered. Though my dad needed me to keep applying pressure to his stab wound, I left his side for a moment and stood next to Josh, ready to blast the intruder with my fire power.

In moments like these, I hated having super hearing. I could hear every single little nerve-racking noise. I heard Josh's sweaty finger slip off the trigger several times. I heard my dad's slow, painful breathing. I heard the twins' teeth chattering with fear. I tried to block everything out and focus on the battle Josh and I were about to fight. But it was hard to focus and tune out the sound of my own overactive heart.

"Whoever comes through that door, I'll handle," I whispered to Josh. "You hang back and protect Dad and the twins."

Josh nodded and tightened his grip. He wasn't about to argue with me about that. I had way more combat training than him. Our mother had trained me herself. I had already gone on five successful missions.

After one more loud crash, a metal figure tumbled through the door.

"Marco!" I yelled running to him. He stood and wrapped me in his strong metallic arms. I had never been so happy to see his metal self in my life. I buried my face in his chest and inhaled. Whenever I hugged Marco in human form, he always smelled like lavender. Probably from the shampoo he used in his long dark hair. But when he converted to metal, his smell was about as inviting as a street lamp. In that moment I didn't care though. I just wanted him to hold me and tell me everything was gonna be all right.

"I am so happy you are okay," he said with his adorably cute accent before mumbling something in French. Then he kissed the side of my head. It was such a soft gentle kiss. I had to admit, I really liked it. But anything more than that wasn't possible for two reasons. First, just from that one little kiss, the side of my head turned to metal for ten minutes.

And second, my mother was trying to kill us all. I think that took priority over any possible make out sessions.

Eight-year-old Ryan flew into the hole that Marco had just created. Literally, he flew. That was his power. When no one else came through, Josh went outside to secure the perimeter. I was still locked in Marco's arms and running my fingers through his long black hair. Hmm, I wondered why his hair never turned to metal as well?

"My mother tried to kill my father. Something is wrong with her." The words flowed out of my mouth uncontrollably fast.

"I know. She came to the safe house too. She took Peter and Katya," he said referring to Ryan's flying twin brother and our Russian mind eraser Katya, who also happened to be Josh's girlfriend.

"Oh, no." I pulled away and wiped the few tears that had escaped. Hopefully, no one else in the room noticed. Superheroes weren't supposed to cry.

"She dragged them right out of their beds and put some sort of device to their head," Marco said. "Their bodies went limp and then she boarded an aircraft with the Selliwood Institute logo. It was all caught on the surveillance camera."

Selliwood. I knew he had to be behind this.

"Why only Katya and Peter?"

"Ryan and I weren't in our rooms. Neither one of us could sleep, so we were in the kitchen having a snack."

"Where's Will Smith?" I asked. Will Smith was actually Specimen W. He was a large white man with a thick German accent, but due to an unholy obsession with the movie *Men in Black*, he preferred to be called Will Smith. He was the first specimen my mother ever rescued. He was like her little brother.

"He went after her," Marco said.

I stared into his green eyes for a moment and then Kyle's face flashed into my head. I realized I still had my arms around Marco's neck. I released him quickly and stepped away. What was I doing? My dad was bleeding to death, my mother was trying to kill people and all I can think of was the next time I'd get to make out with the Tin Man. I had to be the most horrible person in the world.

I thought I noticed a tinge of hurt in Marco's eyes when I pulled away from him and went back to my father. This slipped away when my little brothers ran to him and tackled him with hugs. He picked them up and carried one in each arm.

"We're clear," Josh said, coming back into the storm shelter and clicking the safety on his gun. "How's Dad?" Josh leaned down next to him on the floor.

"He passed out, but his pulse is strong," I said. I leaned down and kissed my dad's cheek. I repeated his instructions over and over in my head. Keep airways open, apply pressure to the wound. Check pulse rate often. With degrees in Biochemistry and Engineering, my dad wasn't a doctor by any means, but he had enough medical knowledge to diagnose himself with a collapsed lung before he passed out. "What are we gonna do Josh? He needs a hospital."

"He doesn't want one," Josh said.

"But he could die."

Josh took a deep breath. A worry wrinkle creased his forehead. He wasn't ready for this type of

13

responsibility. "Let's wait until Will Smith gets back. We'll see what he says."

"And what if he doesn't come back? What if our mother kills him just like she tried to do to Dad? She could have already done it."

"Don't say that Prissy. Mommy's not a killer. She's just sick," Chester said.

"Yeah, the bad guys made her sick," Charlie added.

"They are probably right, Priscilla," Marco said, setting the boys down. "That's the only explanation for why she would suddenly snap like this."

"But how?" I asked wiping sweat off my dad's smooth bald head with a towel. I hoped there was a good reason for why she would attack my father.

"Maybe it has something to do with the machine from Selliwood. The one that stripped her powers," Josh said.

"But that was over five months ago. Why would it suddenly make her crazy now?"

"I don't know, okay?" Josh said, clutching his head in frustration. "I don't know! Just because I'm psychic doesn't mean I have all the answers."

"Josh, it's okay. Calm down. I just asked a question. We'll figure this out together." I reached out and put my hand on his shoulder. "Let's get Dad back in the house."

Marco carried my dad into the house while Josh and I put the twins back to bed. It was hard trying to assure them that everything was going to be all right when we really weren't sure ourselves.

"Does Mommy not love us anymore?" Chester asked.

"Of course she does, Chessie," I said. "You were right before, okay? She's just sick."

"How are we going to make her better?" Charlie asked.

Josh and I looked at each other. That was a good question.

Chapter 3:
Hard Questions

Josh and I took turns keeping an eye on Dad throughout the night. For two hours, I sat at the edge of my dad's bed and watched him breathe. I changed his bandages and tried to make him as comfortable as possible. His breathing was slow and ragged. He only had one working lung. I wondered what that felt like. It had to be painful. Even though my dad was built like a professional wrestler, the whole lung thing had totally incapacitated him. Every once in a while he'd try to take a deep breath and wince. I hated seeing how much pain he was in. I so wanted to take him to get help, but I was trying to respect his wishes.

Sometimes, I wished he was a specimen as well. If he were a genetic experiment like my mother, he would heal much more quickly. I only had half of my mother's mutated genes and I still healed pretty quickly. Back in December when I saved my parents and the other Selliwood kids from the Institute, I had been shot in the shoulder. It had hurt a little, but I had still been able to keep going. And the wound had healed completely in a couple of days.

But my dad didn't have those genes. Instead, he was a normal human. He was a guard at the Selliwood Institute when my mother was a teenager there and that was how they met and fell in love.

Time ticked on slowly after Josh switched places with me. I was exhausted, but part of me didn't want to sleep. I crawled into my bed, but every time I closed my eyes, I saw him lying on the floor of the storm shelter with blood pouring out of his chest. Then I'd jerk awake and rush to his side just to make sure he was still alive.

"Priss, go back to sleep," Josh whispered after the second time I did this. "It's not your turn for another forty-five minutes." He stood up from where he was sitting next to Dad and gave me a hug. "He's gonna be fine," he said into my hair. "I'll come get you if anything happens." Then he sent me that calm feeling that always helped me relax. See, Josh was a psychic and a pretty powerful one at that. He was always able to send me a wave of energy to put me at ease just when I needed it.

After that, I think I fell asleep as soon as my head hit the pillow on my bed. Unfortunately, my sleep didn't last too long.

"Priss, get up. We're going to the hospital," Josh yelled into my room.

I hopped out of bed and threw on my shoes and a jacket. I made it into the hallway just in time to see Josh struggling to hold Dad's body weight.

I took my dad's limp body from Josh and easily carried his three-hundred pound frame through the house and out the front door with my super strength.

18

"What happened?" I asked as Josh held open the door to his truck.

"His pulse dropped. I think he's lost too much blood."

"Why don't we call an ambulance?"

"Because we live in the middle of nowhere. It would take too long for them to even find our house. I think this will be faster."

"What about the twins?" I asked not wanting to leave them alone. They were only five and after the night we'd had, they might flip out if they woke up alone.

Get your father some help. I will take care of the twins, a voice in my head said. It was Marco sending me a telepathic message. Normally, I would have started yelling at him to stop going in my head uninvited, but tonight I was just grateful for his help.

***

When we got to the hospital, Josh wouldn't let me carry Dad inside. It would be too hard to explain why a thirteen-year-old girl could carry a three hundred pound man with ease. Instead, Josh ran inside the Emergency

Room doors and yelled for help. Two men came out of the building and loaded my dad on to one of those rolling bed thingies. That was when all the hard to explain questions started.

"What happened to him?" a nurse asked once we were inside the Emergency Room.

"He was stabbed," Josh said.

"Where?"

"In the chest," I said. "His left lung collapsed."

The nurse looked at me. "How do you know that?"

"I ... um ... He told me," I said pointing to my dad like a three-year-old blaming an imaginary friend for breaking the TV.

"Why wasn't he brought earlier? Where did this happen? Who did this?"

"I ... um ... Help me out here, Josh."

"We ... um," he stuttered. Some help he was.

They wheeled my dad into a room before we had time to answer. Josh and I followed and watched as they worked on him. Seconds later a doctor breezed into the room.

"What have we got here?" she said.

"Stabbing victim. Brought in by a couple kids. Pulse is low and he's lost a lot — He's crashing!"

"Get those kids out of here!"

Someone pushed us out into the hallway. We ended up in the waiting room, huddled together on a couch, both trying not to cry.

"What are we going to do if he doesn't make it, Josh?"

"Don't say that. He's gonna be fine." Josh wrapped his arm around me and hugged me.

"But what if he isn't? What are we going to do? What if they ask us who did it? What are we going to say?"

"I don't know. We'll figure something out."

***

I didn't think it was possible, but somehow I fell asleep right there in the waiting room with my head on Josh's shoulder. What felt like seconds later, he was shaking me awake.

"The doctor is coming," Josh said. I blinked away the sleepiness and was finally able to take in my surroundings as I opened my eyes. We were in a regular old depressing hospital waiting room with the creepy fluorescent lighting and painfully boring white walls. It was daylight now, which meant we had to have been there for at least two hours.

We both stood as the doctor approached us. "How's my dad?" Josh asked.

She held out her hand and said, "I'm Dr. Warner, but everyone calls me Dr. Amy." Dr. Amy looked a lot less like a doctor and a lot more like she should be staying up on the phone all night talking about cute boys and how she was going to buy a new swimsuit with her babysitting money. In other words, she looked really young. But I wasn't going to hold that against her. I mean, I'm sure I probably looked too young to shoot fire out of my fingers. Wait. Was there ever a proper age for that?

Josh shook her hand then repeated his question. "How's my dad?"

"Why don't we have a seat and talk for a minute?" She spoke with a smile but I could see the worry hidden behind her eyes.

"Oh my God. Is he okay? Is he dead?" I started to panic. I would never forgive myself if he was dead. If we had just taken him to the hospital as soon as it happened. Oh, it was all my fault. I should've convinced Josh to take him to the hospital as soon as it happened. If he was dead, it would be my fault.

"No, he's not dead," Dr. Amy said in a reassuring voice.

Josh and I exhaled simultaneously and plopped down into the couch. Dr. Amy pulled a chair directly in front of us and sat down as well.

"He's stable. He survived an emergency procedure to seal the hole in his lung and he's already breathing on his own. Your father is a very strong man."

"Can we see him?" I asked, standing up.

Dr. Amy held up her hand indicating that I should sit back down. "Why don't we give him a few minutes to rest okay? I thought we could talk for a little bit. I'm rather concerned about the condition your father was in. I'm not only concerned for him, but for you. How did he end up getting stabbed? Who hurt him? Where is your mother?"

Josh and I looked at each other. Neither of us responded.

"Are you afraid of someone? Is someone trying to hurt you?"

We still didn't answer.

"Look, the police are on the way. They're going to be asking the same questions I am. I just thought you might be more comfortable talking with me. I'm actually a pediatrician on my ER rotation. I'm used to dealing with kids."

I rolled my eyes. She was not used to dealing with kids like us.

"We appreciate your concern, but we'd really like to see our dad. Can we talk about this later?" Josh said.

Dr. Amy sighed. "Okay, I'll show you to his room."

We followed her down the hallway toward my dad's room. "I'll give you ten minutes with him," she said, "but then I really need some information."

"In ten minutes, we'll tell you anything you want to know." Josh smiled and winked at her. He was such a flirt. Was he really trying to hit on the doctor? She was kind of cute in a bookish kind of way, but she had to be like twice his age.

And what was he talking about telling her anything she wanted to know? We couldn't do that. I was just about to ask him this when I stepped through the door and saw my dad lying in his hospital bed. My normally huge, scary looking father looked small and pale in his bed. I ran to him and threw my arms around him ignoring the wires and beeping monitors.

He groaned. "Where ... am I?"

"We brought you to the hospital, Dad," Josh said.

"Didn't ... I say... no hospitals?"

"We had to, Daddy. You almost died!" I wiped my tears on his hospital gown before anyone could see them. I wanted to be strong for my dad's sake. I didn't want him to know how scared we really were.

"Okay, okay," he said. "But I'm fine now, right?"

"The doctor says you're stable. They sealed the hole in your lung as well," Josh said.

"Great, then I'm good as new. Now, how are we getting out of here?" My dad leaned up on his left elbow and started ripping out needles and cords with his right hand.

"Already? Shouldn't you talk to the doctor first or something?" I asked a little worried. I stepped away from him and crossed my arms. What did he think he was doing? I mean, he'd just come out of surgery. I was pretty sure they'd want to keep him for surveillance or observation or whatever they called it.

My dad flung his legs over the bed and tried to stand. When he got woozy and started to tip over, Josh rushed to his side. They both ended up tumbling onto the bed.

"Let's try that again," my dad said, standing more slowly this time. Josh hopped up, grabbed Dad's clothes and tossed them to him.

"Josh, you're okay with this? Didn't the doctor just say she was coming back in ten minutes and that she wanted answers? We're going to have to figure out a way to explain how Dad got hurt."

"Let's just say Dr. Amy is going to change her mind."

"How?"

Josh shook his head. "You really underestimate me, Priss."

That's when I remembered my brother's special talent. He wasn't a regular psychic that looked into crystal balls or flipped over weird looking cards. No, Josh had the ability to connect with someone's mental wavelength and manipulate it any way he wanted. We called it hypnotic suggestion. Once, he was able to get a group of gun-toting guards to spontaneously gyrate to a Christina Aguilera song. I hoped today's antic would be a little less disturbing.

"Here you go, Mr. Doe," Dr. Amy said as she pushed a wheelchair into the room.

"Doe?" I said, looking at Josh. "You couldn't come up with anything more creative than Doe?"

"Shut up, Priss," was his clever response.

"Your paperwork is all in order," Dr. Amy continued. "I hope you've had a lovely stay." The poor woman sounded like a hotel bellman. I hoped Josh hadn't done any permanent damage to her brain or anything.

As my dad slowly sat down in the wheelchair, Dr. Amy took out a folded slip of paper and seductively slipped it into Josh's back pocket. "Give me a call some time," she said with a toss of her hair.

Josh just smiled and watched her walk out.

I punched him in the arm.

"Ow, Priss. That hurt!"

"Good. You enjoyed that way too much."

Chapter 4:
All Kinds of Chips

Dad slept all the way home from the hospital. Then I carried him to bed and tucked him in just like he used to do to me. Four years ago, when my mom started fighting against the Selliwood Institute full time, my dad became the househusband. He was the one who took us to school, helped us with homework and cooked dinner. For a while, he was both mom and dad. I didn't know what I'd do if I lost him.

When Josh went to take a shower, I used the family computer to type an email to my best friend,

Taiana Houston. She was in Denmark representing the United States in some science competition so I wasn't sure what time it was there. I thought it would be easier to just explain everything that happened in an email instead of calling her and possibly waking her up. I knew she wouldn't mind being woken up. But honestly I didn't feel like explaining everything at the moment. Somehow saying it out loud made it even more real.

No one knew about our little family secret except Tai. We told each other everything. Besides, since she was a genius, maybe she could help us figure out what to do next.

An hour or so later, Josh, Marco, Ryan and I met in the kitchen and tried to come up with a plan.

"So what do we know?" Marco asked, pacing the floor with his hands clasped behind his back. The immediate threat of danger was gone so he had converted back to human form, but he still radiated an intensity that showed just how scary the situation really was. "We know that Q is now working for Colonel

Selliwood again," he continued, "but we don't know why and we don't know how."

I sat at the kitchen table and stared out of the window at the mid-morning sun. I didn't like the way he suddenly started referring to my mother by her Specimen name again. She wasn't Specimen Q anymore, no matter what Selliwood had done to her. She was my mother. She'd always be my mother.

"Maybe it's mind control," Josh volunteered.

I thought about that for a second. "That makes sense," I said, looking at Josh. "When I overheard Colonel Selliwood and Dr. Witherall talking five months ago, Selliwood said that the problem with the specimens was that they thought too much. He said he'd finally figured out a way to control them."

The boys grew silent as they thought about how he could possibly make this happen. My thoughts kept going back to my dad and what my mother had done to him less than twelve hours ago. I was still worried about him, but I couldn't show it. I had to be strong and brave. That's how girls who could shoot fire out of their fingers felt. They didn't feel scared to death and overwhelmed as I did right now.

Little Ryan levitated to the corner of the ceiling and hugged himself. He, too, was upset. He probably felt lost without his twin. I stood up and grabbed a tin of Dad's homemade chocolate chip macadamia nut cookies from the counter. I held them out to him hoping they would make him feel a little better. He shook his head and rejected them. What was I thinking? Yes, the cookies were amazing, but they were no substitute for a lost sibling. No amount of chocolate chips ... chips ... wait a minute.

Suddenly, I remembered a conversation I had with my mother about how she fell in love with my father. She said that while she lived in the Institute, she was once bedridden for a week because of a malfunction with the computer chip in her head. My father, who was a guard at the Institute, came to visit her every day while she was sick.

I dropped the tin of cookies on the floor. Everyone stared at me.

"I think I got it. Chips. Computer chips in ... in ... in your head. All the specimens have microchips in their heads ... my mother's headaches. It all makes sense now." The words were flowing out of my mouth faster than I could control them.

For months, my mother had been grouchy and suffering from constant migraines. When we found out she was pregnant, we all just assumed that pregnancy hormones were causing the problem. But what if it was Selliwood?

"Priss, slow down. What are you trying to say?"

"All of the specimens born or created or whatever at the Selliwood Institute were implanted with microchips in their brains to help further the mutation. My mother told me about them herself. What if Dr. Witherall and Colonel Selliwood figured out a way to use those microchips to control them?"

Marco and Ryan looked at each other. They knew of the microchips I was talking about. They each had one. Ryan even touched the left side of his head self-consciously. I guess he even knew where it was.

"Josh, when you and everyone were kidnapped by Selliwood, they tortured Mom on this machine. All this time, we thought the machine stripped the genetic mutations off of her DNA, leaving her powerless. What if we were wrong? What if that machine just subdued her powers until Selliwood and Witherall were ready to take control of her?"

"That could be why she held a device to Katya and Peter's head. She could have been activating their computer chips," Marco said

Our spirits lifted and crashed at the same time. On the one hand, it was great that we were finally starting to put things together. On the other hand, there was no way we could defeat a device implanted into someone's brain. Not only that, but both Ryan and Marco were at risk for being overtaken and reprogrammed. That was probably what happened to Will Smith. It had been over twelve hours since he left and we hadn't heard anything from him. He was probably now the enemy. Any second, Ryan and Marco could become the enemy as well.

And there was no telling what the microchip was doing to Mom's body. She was nine weeks pregnant with my little sister. Okay, so I didn't know for sure it was a girl, but I could hope right? I couldn't deal with another brother. I had too many as it was. Anyway, what if something happened to the baby?

The one good thing in all this was that Josh and I didn't have computer chips in our brains. Josh and I were safe. For now, anyway.

Chapter 5:
Too Little, Too Late

An awkward silence fell over the kitchen as we stared at each other. We were probably all asking the same questions in our heads. What would happen if we actually had to fight each other? What if we had to kill Katya, or Peter, or even my mother? How long would it take before Selliwood came back for Marco and Ryan?

I closed my eyes and took a deep breath, trying not to think about having to one day fight my friends or my mother. That's when Josh sent me a telepathic message:

Priss, if you're right about the microchips, which I think you are, then we need to keep an eye on Marco

36

and Ryan. We don't know how Selliwood is controlling Mom. Any second he could take them over as well.

I didn't know how to respond to that. First of all, my telepathy sucked. Okay, well, to be honest, it was nonexistent. Mom thought that as time went on I would develop the ability since she and Josh were such powerful psychics. But so far, nothing. Half the time I didn't know what *I* was thinking let alone anyone else. So I really had no way of sending a telepathic message back to Josh. Second of all, I'd hate to think Marco would turn against me.

I opened my eyes and noticed Marco staring at me. Had he heard what Josh said? I still wasn't too sure how this telepathy thing worked some times. Was he able to, like, intercept signals like a transistor radio or something? Or was there some sort of call waiting plan for telepaths?

"I'm going to go check on the twins," Josh said, heading out the door with Ryan right behind him. Ryan would want to make sure the twins were all right as well. Even though he was three years older than my little brothers, they had developed quite a friendship.

Marco was still staring at me.

"What?" I said when I couldn't take it anymore.

He took a step toward me, forcing me to step back as well. It was not like I was afraid of him or anything. I mean, I think I could take him in a fight. I didn't really want to have to find out. I mean, that would be miserable having to fight him. I momentarily wondered if my super strength and firepower could trump the whole metal thing he had going on with his body.

Marco kept coming toward me. His green eyes were so intense they kind of made my heart speed up. If he did intercept the message, was he angry that we thought he could be a danger?

I stopped backing up when my back hit the counter. Marco leaned toward me and said, "I'd die before I obey Colonel Selliwood again." His voice was so deep and powerful it made the hair on my arms stand on end. And his cute French accent actually made my stomach tingle. Just the sight of him made me want to throw on a beret and start spouting out romantic poetry. And I didn't even like poetry ... unless it was backed by a hip hop beat.

"Okay," I said, nodding. I couldn't think of anything more intelligent to say. I was too ... too ... I don't really know what I was feeling. It was like a cross between excitement and anxiety. Let's call it exciety.

Then he leaned toward me even more like he was about to kiss me. He licked his lips and brushed a strand of hair out of my face.

"I will never hurt you," he said before turning and dashing out of the back door.

"I sure hope you mean that," I said to the empty room.

***

It took like ten minutes for me to calm down enough to leave the kitchen. Marco added a whole new level of complications to the situation. I was already worried enough about my mom, Peter, and Katya. Now I also had to worry about Marco's chip somehow being activated. I didn't know if I could emotionally handle him

39

turning against me as well. I didn't mean to fall for him, but I kinda did. I really liked him and I couldn't deny it.

Josh was waiting for me on the couch when I left the kitchen and entered the living room.

"I think Marco knows we're afraid his chip might be activated," I said, plopping next to him on the couch.

"It's a legitimate concern. He should understand," Josh said, crossing his arms and staring at the blank television. "And if necessary, he should be willing to sacrifice himself for the mission."

"Sacrifice? What are you talking about, Josh?"

"Nothing. Look, I'm beat. I'm gonna take a nap." He stood up and started heading to his room.

"Nap? What are you? A kindergartener? There's no naptime for us. Shouldn't we get moving? Shouldn't we do something?"

"There's nothing we can do right now, Priss. We just have to wait."

"Wait? I don't want to wait, Josh," I said, hopping off the couch. "What if we wait too long and then we're too late to save Mom? Dad is stable now so I think we should hop in the jet and go — "

"Go where, huh? We have no idea where she is or where she's taken Katya and Peter."

"But we know Specimen W followed her. We can get in the jet and track the hovercopter. It's only been a few hours."

"It's too dangerous. Who's gonna take care of the twins? Dad's still not completely recovered. We can't just jump into a mission without the proper plan and preparation. I'm the oldest. I'm in charge. I say we wait."

I shook my head and crossed my arms. He wanted me to wait and do nothing while my mother fell deeper and deeper into Selliwood's control. Not to mention Katya and Peter. They were probably getting brainwashed as well. They were probably the enemy by now. And since Specimen W hadn't come back or contacted us, I could only assume the worse happened to him. By the time Josh decided it was time for action, I was afraid whatever we did would be too little too late.

After Josh stormed off to his room, I sat back down on the couch fuming with anger. "He's the oldest, he's in charge," I said in a mocking tone to the empty room. There had to be a way I could get him to see that we needed to act now. But if he didn't see it my way, maybe I'd just have to take action myself.

***

"What is it?" I heard Charlie whisper. At first, I couldn't tell where I was or where they were. Sometimes having super hearing could be really confusing. In my sleepy state of mind, I wasn't really sure if they were right next to me or two rooms away. I peeked out of one eye and noticed that my twin little brothers were standing right over me and staring intently at my neck. I closed my eyes and tried to remember where I was and what I was doing. I must have fallen asleep on the couch after my fight with Josh. He was right about the whole napping thing. I must have been completely exhausted to fall asleep at a time like this.

"I don't know," Chester answered.

"Is it alive?"

"Do you think she can feel it?"

I tried to ignore them, but the more they pointed and stared at me, the more I wanted to know what had captured their attention so much. Was there a bug crawling on me or something?

"We should name it!" Charlie said.

"Yeah, like a pet!"

"We'll call it Spot."

I sat up on the couch so fast both Charlie and Chester jumped back. "All right, that's it. What in the world is going on? What are you looking at?"

"You have something on your neck, Prissy," Chester said.

"Yeah, it's so big I think it's breathing. Maybe it's a tumor."

"What are you talking —" I stopped abruptly when I reached up and touched my neck. No, it couldn't be. I jumped up and ran to the bathroom to try to disprove what my fingers had just felt.

When I clicked on the bathroom light and stared in the mirror, I gasped. There was no way I had just gotten my first pimple.

Chapter 6:
The Pimple

I ran from the bathroom and bumped right into Josh. I tried to cover up the monster growing out of my neck but I wasn't fast enough.

"What is that!" he yelled with a little too much glee in his voice.

"Nothing. Leave me alone." I went to squeeze past him in the narrow hallway, but he blocked my path.

"Good God, it's huge. If your boobs were that big, you might actually need that bra of yours." Josh laughed at his little joke.

My mouth flew open in shock. "Why you little — "
I picked up my big brother, tossed him over my shoulder
and started walking toward the back door. He was still
laughing, but he stopped abruptly once he figured out
where I was going.

"Priscilla, stop! Don't you dare. Priss, put me
down!"

But I ignored him as I headed toward the steaming
pile of manure in the backyard. I had been longing to do
this to him since Dad started collecting the manure to
convert into fertilizer. This was about to be a dream
come true. I did a little spin move then threw him into
the pile like I was doing the discus in the Olympics.
"Take that, Mr. I'm-in-charge."

Charlie and Chester had followed us outside and
started laughing at Josh trying to scramble his way out of
the cow manure.

"Oh, you two are gonna get it too," I said, looking
at them. They screamed and took off running in opposite
directions.

I decided to chase after Chester. I still owed him for a little incident involving my doorknob and some glue. Josh finally got out of the pile and chased after Charlie flinging cow poop along the way.

I caught up to Chester, picked him up and gave him the same fate as Josh. Chester was kicking, screaming and laughing as I tossed him into the manure. Then I felt a sudden shove behind me and before I knew it I was lunging headfirst into the stinky pile as well. Both Charlie and Josh had snuck up from behind and shoved me in. A disgusting, dirty, smelly wrestling match between my brothers and me started. We were laughing so hard we could barely stand up straight. I think we all needed this silly stress reliever after the night we'd been through.

Finally, I noticed Ryan hovering above the pile with his hands behind his back and a confused expression on his face. I looked to my left and Marco was standing there, also looking very confused.

"Do you need assistance, Priscilla?" Marco asked.

"No, we're just having fun," I said.

"Fun? Playing with feces is fun?"

"Well ... not usually ... It's just that ... Um ... " How was I supposed to explain this to him? The Specimens had spent so much time locked away in the Selliwood Institute, only learning how to kill, that they always had a hard time understanding normal human behavior. Okay well, playing in manure wasn't really normal, but either way it was going to be hard to explain. Thankfully, Josh jumped in.

"See, Marco, sometimes when humans get too stressed out, they need something to relieve that nervous energy. Doctors say laughing is the best medicine. Seeing my brothers and sister completely covered in cow manure is quite funny."

"Funny? Hmm." Marco scratched his chin as if deep in thought. "Will it be as funny as this? Now Ryan!" With that, Ryan took his hands from behind his back and starting flinging water balloons at us. Marco pulled out the water hose and completely doused us with water laughing the whole time.

I guess Marco had learned more about human behavior than I thought.

***

After I got cleaned up, I decided I needed to talk to Tai immediately. I didn't care what time it was in Denmark.

"Houston, we have a problem," I said as soon as she answered the phone.

Tai gasped. "Oh, no! Is your Mom back? Did she attack again?"

"You got the email?" My hair was still wet from the shower, so I sat on the bed and started drying it with a towel while holding the phone in place with my shoulder.

"Yeah, I read it over and over again. I can't believe it. Is your dad okay?"

"Yeah he's fine. Josh and I were pretty scared for a while, but I think he's gonna make it now."

Tai breathed a sigh of relief. She was pretty close to my parents. After being kidnapped with them and held at the Selliwood Institute, she was basically a part of the family.

"So what's the big emergency?" she asked once she had calmed down a little.

"Oh it's bigger than big. It's huge. I'd rather be dead right now than have to go through this." I flopped onto my back and threw the towel over my head.

"Okay, now I just think you're being dramatic. Don't have a 'Prissy Fit.' Just tell me what's going on."

"I've got a pimple on my neck," I whispered into the phone just in case Marco was nearby. Thankfully, he hadn't already noticed it during the manure/water fight.

There was a pause.

"And?" Tai said finally.

"And I look like a monster!" I said, leaping from the bed. "This is serious, Tai. It's huge."

"It can't be that big of a deal. You're overreacting."

"Josh is calling it my third boob."

Tai started laughing hysterically.

"It's not funny! Charlie and Chester named it Spot and just asked me if they could pet it."

She laughed harder.

"You better be happy you're my best friend. If you weren't, I'd come over there and toast your insensitive tail right now." I sat down on the bed and started drying my hair with the towel again. Then I realized something. I could shoot fire out of my fingers. Why the heck was I using a towel? With my hand a safe distance away from my head, I lit a flame and then moved it up and down the length of my hair.

"Sorry, Priss. I just don't know what you expect me to do. I'm in Denmark right now. It's not like I can hop on a plane and help you conceal your pimple with makeup or something."

"I don't think makeup would even help. It would be like trying to fill the Grand Canyon one thimble of water at a time. Just plain pointless." With my hair dry, I shut off my flame and started searching my messy room for a hair scrunchie.

"You're probably right. This sounds like more of a stress-induced problem than a cosmetic anomaly."

"Stop using big words and just tell me how to get rid of it!"

"It's on your neck, right? Why don't you just wear a turtleneck?"

I rolled my eyes at her ridiculous suggestion. "You want me, the human fire ball, to wear a turtleneck? I'll spontaneously combust!"

"Well, besides drinking more water and trying to relax, I don't know what else you want me to tell you, Priss. And I don't know how you're supposed to relax with your current mom situation."

I sighed. She was right.

"Look on the bright side," she added. "At least you don't have a big date or anything coming up."

That didn't make me feel any better. It just reminded me of my awful boyfriend troubles. Kyle Montgomery was my first boyfriend. We grew up together back in River's Bend, Pennsylvania. We did everything together from racing each other on our bikes to pranking nearly the entire eighth grade. He was my partner in crime and up for doing crazy things that Tai would never do. But back in February, when I had saved the President's daughter from some kidnappers, Kyle kind of saw me kiss Marco. But I wasn't cheating on him. It totally wasn't like that. See, Marco could transfer his powers with a kiss. He was just trying to protect me before I fought against Specimen Zero. But since Kyle didn't know the truth about my family, we couldn't really explain all that to him. To make things worse, I kind of enjoyed kissing Marco. Okay, I really enjoyed kissing Marco. But that didn't mean I didn't like Kyle too, right? I was so confused.

"Well, Kyle and I might not be together anymore, but what about Marco? I can't let him see me like this."

Tai went silent again. Then she sighed.

"What's wrong?" I asked her. I gave up trying to find a hair accessory and sat cross-legged in the middle of my room.

"If you must know." She paused again then took a deep breath before blurting, "I don't think you should be with Marco."

"Why not?" This was news to me. I don't think we had ever talked about Marco like this before. I had no idea how she felt about him.

"I just don't think he's right for you. I think you belong with Kyle."

"But Kyle hates me. He refuses to talk to me. He sends back all the letters I send to him."

"Priss, Kyle has been in love with you since the third grade, maybe even before that. Do you know he missed almost a week of school after you moved away from River's Bend? He claims he had the flu, but I know it was because he missed you so much."

"Kyle hates school as much as I do. He'd use any excuse to get out of going."

Tai sighed again. "Priss, the boy has got it bad for you. And yes, he can be annoying and moronic sometimes, but when it comes down to it, you two are perfect for each other."

"Wait ... are you calling me annoying and moronic?"

"Priss, I'm being serious here." I could imagine she probably rolled her eyes at this point. "You and Kyle are my two best friends and I want to see you together."

I got quiet for a minute while I let this sink in.

"Now, I don't know Marco too well," Tai continued. "I'm sure he's a perfectly nice guy. And he's admittedly the most gorgeous piece of human I've seen walk the Earth besides your brother but what kind of a future do you two really have together?"

"Whoa. Wait. What did you say about my brother?"

"Come on, Priss. You know your brother is hot."

I gagged a little.

"Anyway, you and Marco can't be together. I mean every time he kisses you, he turns you into metal. What kind of relationship would that be?"

She had a point there.

"Kyle is just really hurting right now. Give him some time. He'll come back to you. I know it."

I wasn't so sure.

"Anyway, let me know when you and Josh have decided on your next step. I want to help, okay?"

"Okay, talk to you later."

After hanging up with Tai, I continued my search through the piles of clothes and comic books on my floor. I didn't find a hair scrunchie, but I did find a turtleneck.

Chapter 7:
The Witherall Locket

At two o'clock in the morning, Josh burst into my room. He was pale, sweating and out of breath.

"Witherall," he said before opening my dresser and flinging out my clothes.

I rolled over and put the pillow over my head, too groggy to try and process what he was talking about. A second later, everything came flooding back to me, though. My mother, Selliwood, the specimens, kidnapping, mind control. This was no time to be worried about sleep. Josh was in my room all panicky and stuff for a reason. The last time he did something

57

like this, he told me to take Marco with me on a certain mission, which ended up saving my life.

"What about Witherall?" I asked while hopping out of the bed. I flipped on the lights and immediately regretted that decision. It was way too bright. I shut my eyes tightly while slapping the wall trying to shut the lights off again. Once I had the switch off, I lit my finger instead. The flame filled the room with a warm glow.

Josh ignored my question and kept digging through my clothes.

"Um, Josh, I don't think you're going to find Dr. Witherall in my panty drawer."

"The locket. Where'd you put the locket?" he asked, moving on to my shirt drawer.

"What locket?" I had no idea what he was talking about. I closed my eyes and tried to concentrate. Witherall. Locket. Did he mean the necklace Dr. Witherall had given me?

A few weeks ago, Josh had a vision that we needed to return to River's Bend for some reason. I didn't argue. I just hopped on the jet and went. When we got there, Dr. Witherall showed up along with Specimen U. I thought we were in for a fight, but instead, he gave me a necklace and told me it was for my birthday. Weird. No, weirder than weird. One second, the man is trying to slice me open for his research and the next he was playing Santa Claus or something.

I shut off my flame and walked over to my bed. I flipped over the mattress and then dug my hand into the small slit I had created. I pulled out the diamond necklace with the large L hanging from the center and dangled it in front of my face. "Is this what you're looking for?" I asked Josh. He turned and walked over to me. Then he just stared at the necklace as if he was afraid to touch it. I lit another flame so he could get a better look. "It's a necklace, Josh. Not a locket."

He shook his head, and then carefully took the piece of jewelry out of my hand. "It's a locket."

He sat on the floor and continued staring at it. After shutting off my flame, I braved the brightness and flipped on the lights again before joining him on the floor.

Josh used his index finger to slowly trace the edge of the red L. When he got to a certain place, he paused and the L popped open. I guessed it was a locket.

"How did you know?" That was a pretty stupid question to ask a psychic, but hey, I was only thirteen and it was two o'clock in the morning. You try thinking straight under those conditions.

"I had a vision," he said, staring closely at the contents of the locket.

"What's inside?"

"Letters." He reached for a notebook that I had lying around my room and dumped the contents of the locket on to it.

R-N-C-G-A

"What does it mean?" I asked, staring at the ridiculously tiny letters. It was like trying to read a grain of rice.

"Maybe it spells something."

We started arranging the letters.

R-A-N-C-G

"That mean anything to you?" Josh asked.

I shook my head and rearranged them again. G-R-A-C-N

"Anything?" I asked.

"Nothing." Josh took a turn and came up with C-R-A-N-G

I stared at those letters for a moment. I got a tingly feeling all over, like something important was about to happen.

"Crang," I said after a moment. For some reason, I was whispering even though my dad was knocked out on painkillers and my little brothers could sleep through a monster truck rally in their room. "Josh, I know that word."

I stood up and started pacing my messy room, nearly tripping over a basketball and a giant Pixy Stix.

"How? From where?" he asked, staring up at me.

"Crang. I've heard that word before. In United Arab Emirates, Xi said something about meeting Dr. Witherall at Crang. And before that, at the Selliwood Institute, Dr. Witherall said he would meet Colonel Selliwood at Crang in order to start the next phase of their plan."

"That must be where they are. That's where they have Mom."

"But Josh, after my fight with Xi in UAE, Dad looked everywhere. There is no place on Earth called Crang. It doesn't exist."

"Yeah, I remember that." He stared at the locket again deep in thought. "It has to exist. This," he said holding up the necklace, "is not a coincidence. Crang exists and we have to find it."

"Well, what are we waiting for? Let's do this."

Josh hopped up and ran out of the room to go get dressed. I threw on a pair of jeans and then decided I needed a little sugar rush for some energy. I popped open my Pixy Stix and chugged half of it. Then I washed it down with a near empty can of Mountain Dew that was sitting on my window sill.

I sat down on the bed waiting for the sugar to kick in while staring at the locket and the tiny letters. The locket that Dr. Witherall had given me. A man who one day wanted to kill me and the next day wants to help me blow out birthday candles or something. Josh was right. There was no way all of this was a coincidence. There was no way he would out of the blue give me a clue-filled locket.

What are you up to, Witherall?

Chapter 8:
Excuse me,
While I Kiss This Guy

Thirty minutes later, Josh and I were in the briefing room of the safe house using every internet search engine known to man trying to find Crang. I never typed so fast or so much in my life. Together, I'm pretty sure we searched every inch of the world for this place. It wasn't a city, it wasn't a state, it wasn't a country, and it wasn't an organization. We started to think it was the name of someone who had connections to Witherall or Selliwood. We found a David Crang on Facebook. But unless Dr. Witherall or Colonel Selliwood spent their free time in Cancun on Spring Break wearing tacky shirts and drinking fruity drinks with umbrellas, we were pretty sure there was no connection.

By seven in the morning, I was exhausted and Josh was cranky. I mean more cranky than usual. He was like super cranky. He slammed his laptop shut and stormed out of the basement without saying a word. It must have been killing him to know that he was helpless in finding Mom or his precious Katya. I started thinking about the awkward beginning to their relationship. Being born and raised in the Selliwood Institute, she didn't really understand the concept of flirting. So when she noticed how my brother always found a way to take off his shirt in front of her, she thought it was because we had a problem with laundry. She had no idea that my brother was trying to hit on her. I finally explained things to her, well, I explained as much as I could without puking, and she got the point. The next time Josh asked her out she accepted and they'd been inseparable since.

Josh didn't have the best luck with girls. His first girlfriend broke his heart and cheated on him. I thought he'd finally found happiness again with Katya. And now

The more time passed, the less chance we

⸺ing her and reversing the programming

Witherall and Selliwood had done.

There had to be something I was missing. I felt like all the pieces were there, but for some reason I couldn't put them together to see the whole picture.

Some of the pieces had been handed to me by Dr. Witherall himself, the same man who drugged my mother and performed genetic experiments on her for seventeen years. The same man who posed as my math teacher and then kidnapped me. Whoa. Wait. What if all those clues were just part of some sort of elaborate trap? I mean, why would he be trying to help us? It had to be a trap. He was just trying to throw us off the right path.

I closed my eyes and tried to go over everything in my mind. I thought about the Institute, my time there, my mother's time there. I tried to focus and see Dr. Witherall handing me the box with the locket. Was there something in his eyes that would give away whether he was friend or foe? Oh, why couldn't I be psychic like Josh? Maybe I would be able to sense his true intentions or something.

I must have fallen asleep because the next thing I remembered was someone tapping my shoulder.

"Good morning, Priscilla," Marco said when I opened my eyes. He was sitting next to me at the briefing room conference table.

"Marco? I didn't even hear you come in," I said with a yawn and a stretch. So much for super hearing, I thought as I stretched my arms above my head. "How long have you been here?"

"A little over an hour."

"You've been watching me sleep for over an hour?" I said while I tried to smooth down my hair. I was sure I looked awful after sleeping facedown on a cold conference table for an hour. But Marco didn't seem to mind.

He nodded. "You are beautiful when you sleep."

I felt my cheeks heat up. I tugged on the suffocatingly (is that a word?) hot turtleneck I wore to cover up my embarrassing pimple situation. I thought I would burst into flames. Why did he have to say things like that?

"So I'm not beautiful when I'm not asleep?" I said with a chuckle, trying to lighten the mood.

"No, that's not what I meant. I —"

"I know, Marco. I'm just kidding."

"Oh, right. I still have to get used to your humor."

He paused for a moment and that was when I noticed a chocolate cake and a glass of milk sitting in front of me. "What's this?" I asked.

"Oh, I made you breakfast," he said with a satisfied grin.

I looked between him and the cake several times. "You made me a cake ... for breakfast?"

"Yes, I made it myself. Don't worry, it is not feces."

"What?" I said my eyes expanding.

"It was a joke. I was just kidding. You know I was referring to you and your brothers playing in the feces."

"Oh, right." I sighed in relief. I couldn't help but smile a little at the gleam in Marco's green eyes. He was learning quickly.

"It is your father's special recipe," he added. "When I saw you were down here sleeping, I went upstairs and made it for you. It's right out of the oven. It is still warm."

I looked at the cake again and raised my eyebrows in surprise.

"You don't believe I can cook?" Marco asked. He was starting to look a little disappointed.

"No, I believe you made it, it's just that it's eight thirty in the morning." I paused. How could I say this without hurting his feelings? "Um, people don't eat chocolate cake for breakfast."

"They don't?"

I shook my head.

"I've seen you eat doughnuts for breakfast, correct?"

I nodded.

"Well, what is the difference between a doughnut and a cake?"

I opened my mouth to dispute him and then realized I couldn't. Why was it acceptable to eat a doughnut for breakfast and not a cake?

"Fair enough," I said with a shrug as I cut myself a slice.

It was definitely my dad's recipe for double fudge peanut butter chocolate cake. I could tell by the hint of cinnamon. Over the past four years, my dad had turned into quite a cook. I really missed him. It was usually him who led these middle of the night research missions in the briefing room. I know he was technically all right and would make a full recovery, but I still couldn't believe how close I was to losing him.

On top of that, my mother was the one who tried to kill him. She was actually working for Selliwood now. I tried to convince myself that she wasn't behaving normally and that Selliwood was controlling her, but it was still too overwhelming to think of my mother as a murderer. My stomach knotted up. I couldn't finish my slice of cake.

Marco turned my chair around so that he was staring directly into my eyes. "We're going to find her, Priscilla," he said as if he had been reading my mind. Well, he probably was. "Everything is going to be okay." He reached out and wiped away a tear that I didn't even know had formed.

"How do you know?" I asked, looking into his eyes. My throat was tight and dry. My voice was barely a whisper as I tried to hold back tears.

Marco didn't answer. He just kept staring at me. I never wanted to be telepathic more than in that moment. I wanted to know what he was thinking. What was going on behind his striking green eyes?

"I shouldn't kiss you," he said after what felt like ten minutes of staring. He leaned toward me. His hand still rested on my cheek.

"People do things they shouldn't all the time," I said. Whoa, that was a great line. How'd I think of that? I gotta write that down.

Marco smiled slightly then pressed his lips to mine. I'd been waiting two months to do this again. The last

71

time we kissed, I didn't really get to enjoy it. I had to fight Specimen Zero right after. This time there were no mutants trying to kill me. There was just Marco and me.

As he pressed deeper, I got a tingly sensation all over my body. Normally that tingle meant you really liked a guy. I did really like Marco, but I knew that tingle actually meant he was transferring his powers to me. In about five minutes, I would turn completely to metal. But in that moment I didn't care. In the next moment I did, though. That was the moment when the nausea started.

I pulled away and covered my mouth, trying to hold back the urge to spew bile and chocolate cake all over the room. "What's wrong?" he asked.

I shook my head and swallowed. "Nothing," I lied. Swallowing a mouth full of puke is definitely wrong.

He shut his eyes and took a deep breath. "My powers are making you sick, aren't they?" It wasn't really a question. He already knew the answer.

"Maybe if we kiss more often my body will get used to the power transfer and it won't make me sick anymore," I said hopefully. I really wanted to kiss him, but I also didn't want to puke all over him. Talk about unsexy.

Marco stood while shaking his head. "I don't think so. Your body is rejecting the foreign antigen in my saliva. The reaction will get more and more severe." He turned away and looked up the stairs. "I'm sorry, Priscilla," he said before storming out of the basement.

Could my life get any worse? The guy I liked made me vomit and turn into a statue every time we kissed. Maybe Tai was right. Marco and I would never work.

Chapter 9:
Love Sick

A few minutes later, Josh scurried down the steps into the briefing room holding two cups of coffee. Once down the stairs, he stopped abruptly and stared at me like I was some sort of alien.

"What?" I asked when he didn't say anything.

No response. He just kept staring.

"Do I have a booger or something? Why are you looking at me like that?" I asked. I touched my neck to make sure my pimple or third boob or whatever was still being covered up. Yep, all clear. I really had no idea what his problem was.

Josh smirked and shook his head. "Been making out with Marco?" he asked, setting the coffee on the table and then plopping down in a chair.

My jaw dropped open. How did he know? Wait a minute. I looked down at my arms. Sure enough, I was completely metal. There was really no way to deny it. Suddenly, my stomach tightened. There was also no way to stop the vomit that was about to spew out of me. Josh grabbed a trash can and held it in front of me just as all the chocolate cake made an unwanted encore appearance.

"Gross," Josh added with a shake of his head. He set the trash can down and went to sit on the other side of the table.

I wiped my mouth on my arms. Not very helpful since metal wasn't too absorbent. I grabbed an old nasty tissue out of my jeans' pocket and wiped my mouth while trying to calm my breathing. "That's it? Just gross?" I panted.

He took a sip of coffee and nodded. "Well it *is* gross. Look at what you just put in that trash can." He looked at the trash can and shivered a little. "I kinda feel bad for you though. It's got to suck having to puke every time you kiss your boyfriend."

A part of me hoped that the more I kissed Marco, the more my body would get used to the effects, but I didn't think that was going to happen. Marco was right. The power transfer was getting worse. I mean the first time he kissed me, I didn't vomit. Sure I'd felt the nausea and all, but I didn't actually turn into a human volcano.

Wait a minute. Did Josh just call him my boyfriend? "Boyfriend?" I said. "He's not my boyfriend, Josh. And if he was, why are you all right with that? I mean why aren't you threatening to beat him up like you did to Kyle?"

Just a few weeks ago, Josh had tried to scare Kyle to near death right before our movie date. He said he wanted to make sure that Kyle understood the meaning of "boundaries" and that he didn't touch me while we were alone in a dark theater. And this was right after my dad had sprayed Kyle's hands with some kind of glow in the dark green concoction so he could track where he placed them, and right before a ridiculously embarrassing episode involving my little brothers, my bra, and a chicken salad sandwich. Don't ask.

Josh shrugged. "I don't think Kyle is right for you. Marco is different." He took another sip of coffee and opened up the laptop so he could get back to his research. I wasn't about to let him off that easy though.

"Whoa. Wait. What are you talking about? How is Marco different?" Okay, so that was kind of a dumb question. I mean, he did just turn me into the Statue of Liberty, so to speak. If that ain't 'different' then I don't know what is.

"Marco is one of us. He knows what we're going through. Kyle will never be able to understand our genetic mutation."

"But we don't know that. Maybe he would understand. I never gave him a chance," I said, banging my metal hand against the table.

Josh sighed. "I just think that in the long run, you might be happier with Marco."

"In the long run?" I asked skeptically. "I'm only thirteen. I'm not planning a wedding or anything."

Josh shrugged and started typing on his computer. I could tell he'd already put the situation out of his mind. He had more important things to think of, like how to get his mom and his Katya back. But I kept thinking about Marco.

"Well, what about the metal conversion thing?" I said a few minutes later. I pointed to myself as evidence. "How are we supposed to be boyfriend and girlfriend if we can't even kiss?"

"You're too young for kissing anyway," he said with a smug smirk.

I gave him a death glare. He'd better be happy I couldn't shoot fire out of my eyes.

"Okay, okay. Don't look at me like that," he said, pretending to hide behind his hands. "We'll figure out something. You and Marco will be together one day. I know it."

Ugh. I hated when he did that. Any time Josh used those words "I know it," I never knew if he meant it in a normal I'm-a-big-brother-and-I-know-everything kind of way or in an I'm-a-freaking-psychic-and-I-know-everything kind of way. Either way, it was annoying.

Now I was completely confused. My best friend thought I should be with Kyle, but my brother was convinced Marco was the one for me. I didn't know what to think.

We fell into silence as Josh got back to work searching the internet. I closed my eyes and waited for the "metal effect" to wear off. Searching the internet again felt pretty pointless. We had been at this for hours and were no closer to finding Mom and the others.

"What if this is all a trap?" I asked Josh an hour later.

"What do you mean?" He turned away from his computer and looked at me.

"The necklace and this Crang thing. What if Witherall gave me that necklace with the letters inside to just put us on a false trail? What if we're just wasting our time?"

"I've thought of that." Josh sighed. He turned his attention back to his computer.

"And?" I said when he didn't keep talking.

"And I don't know what else to do." He stood from the table and ran his fingers through his hair. "Do you know how frustrating this is for me? I'm psychic. I'm supposed to know what happens. I should have been able to stop this before it happened and I couldn't. Do you know how it feels to have no idea what to do next?" He kicked a chair then started pacing the room. "I keep staring at this computer following this Crang lead because it's all I have." Josh closed his eyes and rubbed his temples. "I can't sleep. I can't eat. I can't get Katya out of my mind. Part of me hates Mom for falling into Selliwood's clutches and putting Katya in danger."

"Don't say that, Josh. It isn't her fault. Colonel Selliwood has control of her."

"I know. I know. I know." Josh sat back down and put his head in his hands. "Have you thought about what will happen if we can't reverse Selliwood's programming? Maybe you were right. Maybe we should have gone after them yesterday. We could have used the jet's tracking system to find the hovercopter and Specimen W."

"No, you were right," I said, placing my hand on his back. "We can't just jump into something blindly. We could end up just like Mom, Peter and Katya. We have to have a plan."

Josh shook his head. "What if it's too late for all of them?"

"It's not too late," I said with a confidence that almost convinced me. I stood up and went to his seat. I wrapped my arms around him and said, "We can do this. We *will* do this."

Chapter 10:
That Familiar Dial Tone

We made it back to our house in Missouri a little before lunch. Marco had gone ahead of us so someone besides my dad would be there when the twins woke up. We didn't want the twins crashing into my dad's room and bugging him to play Xbox or get some disgusting gunk out of their hair or something. My dad still needed to rest.

When Josh and I entered the kitchen, Marco was wearing an apron and making peanut butter and marshmallow sandwiches for the twins. Something about a muscular teenage superhuman in an apron made me smile. He was the perfect combination of sweet and masculine.

"Hello," he said, not taking his eyes off of where he was spacing out the marshmallows evenly on the bread.

"Hi," I said awkwardly. I didn't need to be stuck in a room with Marco right now. My feelings were just too confusing. I mean I really wanted to be with him, but that wasn't physically possible. And what about Kyle? I turned to dash out of the kitchen and ended up running right into Josh.

Josh wrapped an arm around me and patted my head. I think he understood what I was going through.

"The phone's for you," he said, letting me slide past him.

What was he talking about? The phone wasn't ringing. And I had super hearing. I would know. "You okay, Josh? The phone's not ... oh." I said as the phone started ringing.

Josh winked at me and said, "It's Tai. You better take it. I think it's important."

I shook my head in amazement as I walked to my room. Josh was getting more and more powerful every day. I just wished his powers would be more useful than a human caller ID.

"Priss, you have to talk to Kyle," Tai said when I picked up the phone. She sounded nervous. This made *me* nervous.

"Why? What happened?" I sat on my bed and folded my legs beneath me. I stuck my thumbnail in my mouth and started chewing. I winced when I realized I had already chewed that nail away and was now sinking my teeth into my flesh. I knew something was wrong and I knew it had to be big.

"Max is dead."

I dropped the phone. I needed both hands to wipe away the bucket of tears that suddenly started pouring out of my eyes. I couldn't take anymore. This was the last straw or the straw that broke the camel's back. Why did both of those doom-filled sayings involve straws? From my experience, straws were actually pretty helpful little things, not harbingers of disaster.

Max was our dog. Kyle's and mine. We found him abandoned by the river when we were eight. We both fell in love with Max at first sight and decided to share him. We named him after my middle name, Maxine, and Kyle's last name, Montgomery. He was kind of like our child. We even had joint custody. Max would spend a month with me and then a month with Kyle. That was until about a year ago when the devil twins perfected their game of Snot Wars with Max as the target. The poor traumatized dog ran away to Kyle's house, never to return. So, after that, I had to go to Kyle's house to visit Max.

"Priss? Are you there, Priss?" Tai asked. My super hearing kicked in and I heard her even though the phone had fallen under the bed.

"I'm here," I said, picking it up. "I can't believe I'm crying. It's just a dog."

"You know good and well Max wasn't just a dog. Just like Kyle wasn't just a boyfriend."

I nodded as if she could see me. She was right. Max was more than a dog and Kyle was more than a boyfriend. Why is it you never think your first pet is ever gonna die just like you think you'll be with your first boyfriend forever and ever?

"When did he die? What happened?" I asked.

"Two days ago. He was hit by a car."

The tears swelled again. I hoped Kyle wasn't there to see it happen. I didn't even want to ask about that.

"Two days ago? And you're just telling me now?"

"Well, you've kind of had other things to deal with. Besides I just found out. Spencer called me. He says Kyle hasn't been to school since it happened. Priss, you have to talk to him. He's completely devastated. In one month, he's lost his girlfriend and the dog he shared with said girlfriend. You're the only one that can help get him out of this funk."

Spencer was Tai's boyfriend. Well, kind of her boyfriend. I wasn't quite sure. It was a long story. See, I used to have a huge crush on Spencer before I fell for Kyle and before I knew that Spencer had a thing for Tai. I still wasn't really sure how Tai felt about him though so

I wasn't sure if they were official or not. Anyway, the situation had to be serious if he called Tai for help.

"I've tried to talk to him. I've called him so many times the numbers are wearing off my phone. He hangs up on me every time."

"I can fix that. You don't have a genius best friend for nothing. Hold on."

The phone went silent for a second. The next thing I heard was Kyle's voice.

"Hello? Tai? Are you there?" he said.

Tai must have had him on the other line and then just connected him over to me. He probably had no idea I was even on the phone. If he did, he would've hung up on me already.

I froze. I didn't know what to say. Of course, there were a million things I *wanted* to say. I wanted to tell him that Marco only kissed me to protect me and that it didn't mean anything. Except, I couldn't say that. For one thing, the kiss did mean something. I didn't want to admit it, but it did. For another thing, I couldn't physically say anything at all in that moment. It was like my throat had swollen shut.

"Hi Kyle," I finally squeaked out.

"Priss?" I couldn't tell whether he was angry, annoyed, or relieved. Maybe he was all three. Tai must not have told him what she had planned.

"Don't hang up," I said quickly. I braced myself for that familiar dial tone. When it didn't come, I took a deep breath and said, "I'm sorry."

"For what?" he said still using angry/annoyed/relieved voice.

"For everything, but especially for Max."

He still didn't hang up. This was a good sign. He was actually letting me talk. "I know you really loved him. I — I did too." That was the truth. That dog was a part of our family. The Kyle and Priss family.

"Sometimes love's not enough," he said. He didn't sound angry or annoyed anymore. Just sad. I closed my eyes and pictured his blond hair that was always perfectly styled even after a thirty minute game of one-on-one basketball. Was it weird that one of my favorite things about him was his hair?

What did that mean? Was he saying he loved me, but that it wasn't enough for us to be together? How could he love me? How could he possibly know if he loved me? He was only thirteen! Did I love him? Was that what this burning in my chest was right now? Was it love? Or did I love Marco? Or was I too young to know the difference?

"I gotta go, Priss," he said, but he didn't hang up. I felt like he wanted to say something else. "I threw a stone for you," he said finally.

I knew exactly what he was talking about. Every year on the first day of Spring Break, we'd have a picnic by the river and then throw stones. Of course, it always turned into a competition and we'd see who could throw the stone the farthest or make it skip the most. It was a silly little tradition we'd started when we were nine. Kyle and I had lots of stupid traditions. Besides Tai, he was my best friend in the world. I was just as shocked as anyone last December when I realized I liked him as more than just a friend.

"I miss you, Priss. I miss you so much it hurts."

"I—I ... " Once again, I didn't know what to say, so I said, "I don't know what to say."

"Say that you miss me too and that you don't want to be with Marco and that we can be together again just like old times."

"I — I." I kept stuttering. I could hear my heart beating in the silence. A silence that seemed to last longer than Josh holding a high note from Christina Aguilera's part in *Lady Marmalade*.

"You know what sucks the most, Priss?" he said, breaking the silence. "What sucks more than watching you kiss another boy right in front of me and more than watching our dog die?"

Oh no, he had seen Max get killed. How awful! I had to fight back tears again.

"What sucks the most is that I really want to hate you ... but I can't."

"Kyle —"

90

"I gotta go," he said and hung up.

"I've missed you too," I said to the dial tone.

Chapter 11:
Ian the Australian

I cried myself to sleep that night. All the boys in the house probably thought I was having my period or something because none of them bothered me. They stayed away like I had some sort of contagious disease. Or maybe Josh had sensed that I needed some alone time and told everyone to stay away. In any case, I was glad they all just left me alone and let me cry.

But when the silent alarm woke me up in the middle of the night, crying was the last thing on my mind. And I think my heart stopped for a minute. I was so nervous I thought I was going to puke. The last time the silent alarm went off, my mom had attacked us and nearly killed my dad. Suddenly, I was very thankful that Ryan and Marco decided to spend the night. What if my mother had come back and brought reinforcements, namely, Peter and Katya? Josh and I wouldn't be able to handle them alone. We were stupid for staying. We should have abandoned the house and ran at the first opportunity.

The alarm was only silent for most people. I could hear it clearly with my super hearing. It set off a light in Josh's room and vibrated the twins' beds so that everyone knew there was danger.

By the time I made it into the hallway outside my parent's room, everyone was already gathered.

Priss, take the twins to Dad's room. Marco, Ryan and I will see what the intrusion is, Josh ordered telepathically.

"No way," I whispered. "I have more combat training than you. You protect Dad and the twins. I'm going in." Before he could argue, I took off toward the living room. Marco and Ryan were right behind me.

As soon as we reached the living room, I heard the clanging of pots and pans. "Kitchen," I said to the boys. Ryan levitated and glowed preparing for a fight. Marco had already started his conversion to metal.

Standing in front of the kitchen door, I kicked through it and jumped inside. Instead of finding a deadly Selliwood Specimen ready to attack us, I found a naked teenage boy shivering behind a frying pan. Yes, naked as in no clothes and only a frying pan away from complete embarrassment.

"Who are you?" I yelled as I covered my eyes.

"Ian!" Marco said. I peeked through my fingers just enough to see Marco step toward the intruder with a smile. He had his arms outstretched as if ready for a hug, but then noticing the boy's naked state, he dropped his arms and stepped back. The metal conversion was starting to reverse so I guess the naked boy wasn't a real threat.

"I'll get his clothes," Ryan volunteered as he flew out the back door.

I was completely confused. "Whoa. Wait. What is going on here? How do you know this naked kid? And why are you so okay with him being, well, naked?"

"Sorry, Priscilla. I'm gonna need to get dressed first, so unless you wanna watch ... " the naked boy said with a smile and an extremely Australian accent. At least, I thought it sounded Australian. How was I to know for sure?

"Priscilla? How do you know my name?" I turned to Marco and said, "How does he know my name?"

"We will explain everything in a moment. Just let Ian get dressed first," Marco said, placing a hand on my shoulder and guiding me out of the kitchen. Then he picked up the door and leaned it against the frame.

Once in the living room, I paced in front of the couch. I was too confused to be angry or scared or anything. I really just wanted to know who this Ian person was and what he had to do with nudity and my kitchen. My mind flashed back to my first and only image of him. I would never be able to use that frying pan again.

"What's going on?" Josh asked, coming into the living room holding one of Dad's revolvers.

"There's a naked dude in the kitchen."

"What?"

"Did I stutter? Naked. Dude. Kitchen."

"Ooo-kaaay?" he said skeptically as he clicked on the safety to the gun. Then he closed his eyes and took a deep calming breath. He was probably trying to use his telepathy to get more information on his own. With his eyes still closed, he took another deep breath and sighed. "Katya," he said.

Great, we were being attacked by naked people and all he could think about was his girlfriend. I rolled my eyes and plopped down on the couch.

Seconds later, I heard an "all clear" from Ryan. I hopped up and followed Josh into the kitchen.

"Okay, so what's going on here?" I asked just as Marco was giving the formerly naked stranger a big macho bear hug. I didn't get a good look at him before so I took a second to study his appearance. Shoulder length hair so blond it almost looked transparent poked out of a big tan cowboy looking hat. He was a few inches taller than Marco and he had a rugged manly air about him that made me think he was older than Marco as well. I wondered how they knew each other. Maybe they were friends in France.

"Good to see 'ya, mate," the clothes-challenged Australian said once they released each other. He sure didn't sound French.

"It's been a long time," Marco said.

The Australian looked around the room briefly then settled on Josh. He walked over to my brother and stretched out his hand. "You must be Josh."

"It's good to finally meet you, Ian," Josh said.

"Whoa, whoa, whoa. Wait a minute here. Am I the only one who doesn't know this guy? Does anybody want to explain to me why there's a psycho Australian in my kitchen?"

Ian the Australian turned to me and said, "Hey, I'm offended by that. I'm not Australian. I'm Kiwi."

I threw my hands up in the air. "Great, now he thinks he's a fruit." I rolled my eyes, crossed my arms and leaned against the refrigerator.

Everyone started laughing which really annoyed me. What was so funny?

Ian took off his cowboy hat, held it to his chest, and then he held out his hand as if asking for a handshake. I looked around skeptically. Josh gave a slight nod as if to tell me it was okay so I reached for the Australian's hand. Instead of shaking it, though, he brought the back of my hand to his lips, stole a glance at Marco and winked.

"You were right, mate. She's a pretty little Sheila." He gave Marco a devilish grin. Marco crossed his arms and glared at him. "Still can't take a joke eh, Marco? Lighten up."

What an annoying little flirting jerk! "Sheila? What do you mean Sheila?" I snatched my hand away from him. "I'm Priscilla. I thought you already knew that."

Once again, I had apparently said something really funny. Everyone started laughing ... again.

I held out my hand and lit a warning flame. "That's it. Somebody better start talking or I'm gonna *light* something up all right." I probably shouldn't have done that. I mean, I had no idea who this guy was. What if he didn't know anything about our mutations or the Selliwood Institute? I could be revealing our secret to a potential enemy. But from the way everyone was laughing, I had the feeling he wasn't an enemy. I also had the feeling he was one of us.

"Oh and feisty, too. Ya sure you can handle her, Marco?"

I aimed a flame and blew the hat right off his head with one thrust of my index finger. "Nobody *handles* me," I said.

"Fair enough," he said. "Let me properly introduce myself. I'm Ian. Katya's twin brother."

Chapter 12:
Fine, Ian from New Zealand

Well, that kinda made sense. I did remember Katya telling me she had a twin brother. And he did have the same white-blond hair. But the similarities ended there. I mean Katya was so straightforward and uptight she reminded me of tall blonde robot. This kid seemed like a wannabe Romeo wrapped in a Crocodile Hunter shell.

And I thought Katya said her brother lived in New Zealand, not Australia. Well, wherever this kid was from, it didn't explain one thing.

"Fine, you're Katya's brother. But why in the world were you naked in my kitchen?"

"The door was locked," Ian the Australian said as he tucked his white button down shirt into his jeans.

I looked around the room once again confused. To everyone else, this was apparently an acceptable answer.

"You hungry, buddy?" Ryan asked.

"Starving."

"I'll make you a sandwich," Josh offered.

"Hello!" I said, waving my hands in the air trying to get everyone's attention. "No one else finds it strange that a teenage boy shows up naked in our kitchen and his only explanation is that our door was locked? I mean, is this a common habit? Are all the boys in Australia doing it?"

"I told you before, Sheila. I'm not Aussie, I'm Kiwi."

"And I told you before; my name is Priscilla, not Sheila. What does that even mean? Kiwi. Are you insane? A kiwi is a little, brown, furry fruit."

"Priss, it means he's from New Zealand, not Australia," Josh said as he moved me out of the way so he could open the fridge. He pulled out some leftover ham and reached for the bread.

"Whatever," I said, crossing my arms. I was still kind of annoyed at how everybody laughed at me before. I felt like there was some secret little boys club meeting happening right in front of me but I didn't have the secret boy decoder to figure out what they were saying. It was totally frustrating.

"And the nudity has to do with his specific genetic mutation," Marco said, holding out a chair for me to sit down at the breakfast table.

After I sat down, he didn't add anything else, so I said, "Well, what's his power? Do his clothes just melt off at the sight of locked doors? I'll guess he'll never be a locksmith."

Ian smiled. "That's not quite it. See, I can walk though solid objects —"

"Yeah, but his clothes can't!" Ryan added with a laugh.

Ian blushed a little and nodded. "It's true. When I walk through a wall, for example, my clothes stay on the other side. I usually don't use my powers because of the nudity issue. I'm just worried about Katya." He sat down across from me. "We usually talk every day telepathically. Three days ago, I lost my connection with her. I know something is wrong. Where is she? Where's my sister?"

***

We all took turns filling Ian in on the events of the last three days. It still hurt to say it was my mother who kidnapped Peter and Katya and who stabbed my dad. Somehow I wished it was all a dream.

Ian just nodded as he listened while finishing off three ham sandwiches, four glasses of milk and all the cookies in the house. I wondered if overeating was another one of his super powers.

"So what's the plan? How do we get my sister back?" Ian asked Josh once we had explained everything.

It kind of annoyed me the way he directed his question to my brother and just ignored the fact that I was even there. Why did he just assume Josh was in charge? Maybe I already had a plan or something. Okay, I didn't, but he didn't even consider the possibility.

"Actually," Josh said, rubbing the back of his neck. "I think you should ask Priss. She should be in charge of this mission."

"I should be?" I said a little shocked. He hadn't told me about this. I quickly covered and pretended to be confident in my abilities by saying, "Yeah, that's right. I should be. I mean, I am. I'm in charge of this mission." I crossed my arms and puffed out my chest a little proud of the fact that Josh had so much confidence in me.

Ian looked back and forth between Josh and me a couple of times before saying, "You can't be serious. She's too young. And she's a girl. How can you put a little sheila in charge of this? There's too much on the line."

"Oh, your butt's gonna be on the line if you call me Sheila one more time," I said, standing up so fast my chair fell to the floor. I didn't know what it was but something about this kid irked me. And this wasn't like a cute, flirty kind of irking. When Kyle and I used to fight, I always knew that deep down I thought of him as a friend. Nothing about Ian said friend to me.

Josh put a hand on my arm to calm me down. He picked up my chair then guided me back to my seat. "She might be a girl and she might be young, but something tells me, she has to be the one to take the lead on this. I can't explain why. I just know that Priss has to be in charge," he said.

Ian shook his head as if he didn't believe my brother. "I don't know how you people do things over here, but there's no way I'm putting my sister's life in a little girl's hands."

"You have no idea what these hands can do," I said, staring him down. Then I lit both my hands on fire for effect. I don't know how long we were locked in this death glare, but I refused to be the one to break it first.

Finally, a cocky smile spread across Ian's face. He leaned back in his chair and cracked his neck. I had won the staring match! Ha! I shook out the flames and leaned back in my chair. I leaned back a little too far and almost fell over. Thankfully, Josh was there to catch me. Yeah, that kinda ruined the effect I was going for.

Ian yawned and said, "Well, I'm knackered."

"Knackered? What does that mean?" I asked.

"You are free to join Ryan and me in the guest room," Marco said.

"Nah, I think I'm going bush."

"Going bush? What does that mean?" Was this kid even speaking English? "Oh no, does that mean he's gonna take his clothes off again?" I covered my eyes just in case.

"And you want her in charge of the mission?" Ian shook his head. "It means I'm tired and I'm going to have a sleep under the stars," he added.

"I'll join you," Ryan said. "Let me grab a sleeping bag."

"I'm gonna make sure the twins went back to sleep," Josh said after Ryan and Ian left.

I sat at the breakfast table drumming my fingers trying not to explode with anger. I really didn't like this Ian kid. I hoped he didn't have to come with us when we went to save the others.

After a few minutes of fuming, I noticed Marco was still in the kitchen with me.

"He's really not so bad once you get to know him," Marco said.

"I really don't even want to find out," I said, rolling me eyes.

Marco and I fell into an awkward silence. He clasped his hands together and stared at his thumbs while I continued drumming my fingers.

"Are you feeling better?" he asked finally breaking the silence. "I know you were crying earlier. I wanted to talk to you then, but Josh said not to."

I had to remember to thank Josh later for that.

"Yeah, I'm fine. Just dealing with some stuff back in River's Bend."

"Kyle?" he asked.

I nodded without looking at him. I didn't want to see that sad look in his green eyes that he got whenever I talked about Kyle.

"He wants you back, doesn't he?"

I nodded again.

"What are you gonna do?"

How could he ask me something like that? How the heck was I supposed to know what I wanted to do? I was only thirteen!

I took a deep breath and said, "First, I'm gonna save my mother." I turned and looked at him. "Everything else is gonna have to wait."

I stood up from the table and went back to bed.

Chapter 13:
The Uh-huh Chorus

After Ian, Ryan and Marco went to sleep in a bush under the stars, or whatever, I went and paced my bedroom. I was still fuming over that Australian idiot. Ugh, he made me so angry. I couldn't believe he was Katya's twin. Katya was a sweetheart. A little stiff and naive but still a sweetheart. How could she even stand him?

I wish she was here now. I would beg her to erase the memory of him from my mind.

I just had to talk to Tai. After our last conversation, I set another watch to her time so I would know when I could call her. According to the watch, it was just after eight in the morning in Denmark. Not only would Tai be awake, she'd probably already eaten, showered, and written a textbook by then.

"Tai!" I screeched as soon as she answered the phone.

"What was it?" She was panicked again.

"Could my life get any worse?"

"Is this about your mom?"

"No."

"Kyle?"

"No."

"This better not be about that stupid pimple."

"No, it's worse. Much worse." I started filling her in on the details of the night as I paced my bedroom and twirled the telephone cord around my finger. Yes, we still had a phone with a cord. We were probably the last family in America without a cordless phone but Dad thought it was too easy to intercept transmissions from wireless phones. Whatever.

Anyway, I told Tai everything about last night, including the naked Australian. But apparently, Tai wasn't

too interested. She barely said a wo
"I'm so sick of being surrounded by
rude, nude, flirting idiot with an annoyin

"Uh huh," Tai said.

"And he keeps calling me Sheila. What's up with that?" I asked while walking in circles around my room. The long telephone cord was wrapped around my waist three times. I nearly tripped over my feet.

"Uh huh," she said again.

"One good thing is that Josh has put me in charge of the mission to save Mom and the others," I added, even though I had the feeling she wasn't really listening. "It's nice to know that he has confidence in me, but he still won't let me just get in the jet and go already. He thinks I'm rushing it."

"Uh huh."

"I started to think he was right for a little while. I mean, we don't know where to go so I would be like flying blind. Anything is better than sitting around doing nothing, though."

"Un huh."

"But if I'm in charge and it's my mission, who says I have to wait to get his 'okay'? Maybe I should just go. What do you think?"

"Uh huh."

"Tai, are you even listening to me?" I asked when I got tired of her chorus of uh huh's.

"What? Oh yeah totally. I was totally listening to you."

"Really? So you're okay with me getting Marco's face tattooed on my butt?"

"Wait, is that what you said?"

"No, it's not what I said. But it proves you weren't listening to me." I tried to unravel myself from the telephone cord and somehow ended up making it worse. How was that even possible?

"Oh sorry, Priss. I'm a little distracted."

Suddenly, I felt a little selfish. Here I was blabbing away about my problems and I hadn't even asked her how she was doing. She was all alone in another country taking some crazy hard science test. I bet she was homesick or something.

I stopped twisting around in circles for a second and said, "Sorry, Tai. I should've asked how your day was going."

"Uh huh," she said, getting right back to her uh huh chorus.

"Tai!" I screamed into the phone trying to get her attention. "You wanna tell me what's going on?"

"Don't be mad," she said after a second or two. That's never a good sign. Whenever someone started a story with the words "don't be mad," it usually meant you were about to get really, really mad. I mean, no words can plop more fear in your gut except maybe "I think we should talk" from your boyfriend or "Is this poisonous?" from your little brothers.

I tried to prepare myself for the worst. Maybe in an attempt to get Kyle and me back together, she'd told him where we lived and he was on his way. See, even though Kyle had been to visit me several times, Dad thought it was too dangerous for him to know our location. So after every visit, Katya erased his memory.

There was no telling how many of Kyle's poor brain cells we killed.

I went to sit down on my bed, not realizing that the phone cord was wrapped around my right foot. I tripped and fell face forward into a basketball that was lying in the middle of my floor. I yelled in pain, but Tai didn't even notice. She just started talking away.

"Remember when your family and I were kidnapped and taken to the Institute?"

When Colonel Selliwood kidnapped my family, they mistakenly took Tai instead of me. She was in my bed covering for me while I was out with Kyle.

"Tai, how could I forget that? That would be like forgetting my foot got ran over by a bus," I said while rubbing my forehead from where it hit the basketball. I probably had "Rawlings" permanently branded on my forehead.

"And remember how I was able to figure out how to get Josh's inhibitor off so that he could help you defeat the guards?" she asked, ignoring my sarcasm.

The inhibitor was this collar-like thingy that they put on Josh and Mom to keep them from using their powers. After I rescued them, I went back into the Institute to save the other Specimens being held against their will. Tai figured out how to get it off of Josh. So when I was up against a room full of guards, Josh was able to use his hypnotic suggestion against them in order to help me out.

"Uh-huh," I said, borrowing her favorite word of the last ten minutes.

"Did you ever wonder what happened to those collars?"

I thought back to that night. Once the institute blew up and the collars powered down, the kids yanked off their collars and threw them into the fire. Mom and Josh were already at the jet. I never thought about what happened to their collars.

"I took them. The inhibitors that were on Josh and your mom, I took them."

"Why?" I wasn't angry or anything. Just a bit confused. What would she want with a couple of

115

glowing contraptions that can completely wipe out my powers?

"I took them so I could study them. I took them apart and I studied them."

"And?"

"And I completely understand their composition."

"And?" I was having a hard time figuring out what this had to do with me and how it was going to help me get a naked Australian out of my house.

"And I think, no, I know how to get your mom, Peter, and Katya back."

Chapter 14:
Crang Revealed

After talking to Tai, I tried to go back to sleep. It was easier than I thought. All the stress must have been wearing me down, because I was out quicker than a Pittsburgh Pirate at bat.

Unfortunately, what felt like seconds later, I awoke to Charlie and Chester standing next to my bed in their matching SpongeBob Square Pants pajamas. I jumped up so quickly I hit my head on the headboard. My poor forehead was really taking a beating tonight. I lay back down and threw my pillow over my face.

"What do you want?" I asked, trying not to sound as annoyed as I really was.

"We can't sleep," Charlie said. Chester nodded in agreement.

"So?"

"When we can't sleep, Mommy or Daddy usually read to us," Chester said. Charlie nodded in agreement.

"So?"

"Will you read to us, Prissy?" Chester asked.

"Please?" Charlie added

How could I deny them? If I was stressed out by the current situation, they had to be scared out of their little five-year-old minds. I sighed and rolled out of bed.

Lately, the twins hadn't really been into stories. They preferred it if someone read to them from a toy catalogue. I picked up a copy of their latest one and started reading out the different types of toy monster trucks available. I ended up reading through three catalogues, but they finally fell asleep by the time I started describing the Big Wheel Bone Crusher 3000.

Once they were asleep, I started spying out their room. The twins were notorious for snatching my things and hiding them in their room. After about five seconds, I spotted one of my *Batman* comics, my Wonder Woman notebook, and my stuffed killer whale that was a souvenir from when we went to Sea World. They had even managed to snag my globe. Sneaky little monsters. I grabbed all my belongings and headed out of the room. That was when I ran into Ian from New Zealand in the hallway.

"It's like six o'clock in the morning. Why are you even awake?" I yelled, completely forgetting my brothers had just fallen asleep. I hugged my stuff tighter and tried to scoot past him.

"I live on a farm. I wake up with the sun," he said coolly.

He seemed smug. Just the sound of his voice made me itch. "Did you wake up with the attitude, too?

Ian smiled. "What you think is attitude is just my Kiwi charm."

I rolled my eyes and continued to try to get past him. Kiwi charm? That sounded like a cereal. I wonder if that was what they ate back in Australia.

119

I didn't really care where he was from as long as he went back ... and soon.

He stepped to the side and blocked me. "Look, sheila. I think we got off on the wrong foot. How about a truce, mate?"

"I'm not your mate and I'm not your sheila. So, you can take your truce back with you to your farm in Australia."

Ian clenched his jaw. Then he snatched the globe out from my arms causing all my other stuff to fall to the floor.

"Look at this," he said, pointing to the globe. "Australia. New Zealand. Australia. New Zealand. Two different countries."

I shrugged. "So? Close enough."

He turned the globe around in his hands. "Look here. Canada. United States. Canada. United States. How would you like it if I called you Canadian all the time?"

I stared at the globe for a minute. Something was starting to click in my mind.

"Priscilla, what's wrong?" Ian asked when I didn't answer him after a few seconds. I took the globe out of his hands, forced my way by and sat down on the living room couch unable to speak. "Was it something I said?"

"Shh!" I said. I had to concentrate. There had to be a reason why the mention of Canada made me all tingly and I'm sure it wasn't because I thought maple leaves were creepy. Cause they were, you know. That flag of theirs was ridiculous. Just a big red leaf looking like a hand about to grab you. I mean, why would they put a leaf on their flag? Who in the world would be afraid of a leaf unless there was something sinister behind it? That leaf was up to something.

But no, it wasn't the leaf thing. Thinking of Canada made me all tingly because it reminded me of Specimen Xi. The first time I fought that psycho Chinese girl with the British accent was in a museum in Montreal. I was protecting a high-ranking official who had ordered Colonel Selliwood to stop some illegal research he was doing at the North Pole.

I looked at the North Pole on the globe. It had to be really cold up there. Once again, I thought of Xi. When I fought her in United Arab Emirates, she took a phone call from Dr. Witherall right in the middle of our fight. She said she didn't want to go back to Crang because it was too "bloody cold." But that didn't really mean anything. I mean, it was cold in a lot of places. I was sure it was just as cold in Russia and Norway and Alaska and all those places near the north pole. Wait a minute. That was it.

"I know where Crang is!"

Chapter 15:
Check Mate

I ran into the kitchen with Ian right behind me.

"Priss, what is going on?" he asked. I just ignored him as I pushed through the door. I think I accidently knocked it off its hinges ... again.

"Crang!" I yelled to Josh, Marco and Ryan. "They're at Crang."

"We've already been through this, Priss," Josh said. He rolled his eyes then rested his head on the table. He was completely exhausted. I wondered if he had gotten any sleep at all. "There's no such place as Crang," he continued with his head still down. "We've already spent hours looking for it. It doesn't exist."

"No, Josh, listen." I put my right hand on his shoulder. The globe was tucked under my left arm. "You were right. I needed to go to United Arab Emirates that night," I said, referring to the mission that turned out to be a trap. Josh knew all along that it was a set up and that there wasn't a sheikh that needed to be saved, but he always stood by the fact that I had to be there at that specific time for some reason. We never knew why and now I did.

"I figured it out. The reason I needed to be in UAE. I was supposed to hear Xi make plans to meet Dr. Witherall at Crang. And then she complained about it being cold up there."

"So? It doesn't change the fact that Crang doesn't exist." He stood up and ran his fingers through his hair. "We haven't been able to find it on a map or any search engine on the internet. Maybe they said ... Clang or Crane or something." Josh wasn't convinced that I had figured something out. He started pacing the kitchen nervously while Ian, Ryan, and Marco stared at me waiting for me to explain this brilliant discovery I thought I had. And, oh yeah, it was brilliant.

"We had it wrong. Crang isn't a country or a state or a city or anything like that. It stands for something. Check it out." I held up the globe for him. Marco, Ryan and Ian leaned in to get a better look as well. "Canada, Russia, Alaska, Norway, Greenland," I said, pointing to each of the places on the globe. "C-R-A-N-G. Crang. Those are the countries that border the Arctic Circle. Selliwood and his people are in the Arctic Circle!" The boys stared at the globe more closely as they processed the possibility. "And remember the first time I fought Xi? I was protecting Pierre Marchaud. He threatened to shut down Colonel Selliwood because of some illegal research he'd been doing at the North Pole. The North Pole is in the Arctic Circle. He must have been building a base."

The boys were quiet as they continued to stare at the globe. "That makes sense," Marco said finally.

"I can't believe she solved the mystery. Good on ya, mate!" Ian said slapping me on the back.

"You can check that mate," I said, squirming away from him. "Don't ever touch me again."

Josh nodded as he continued to stare at the globe. I could almost see relief wash over him. Instead of jumping for joy like most people would, his knees kind of wobbled a little like he was about to faint. I knew my brother though. That was a good reaction. He knew I was right and he agreed with me. "You figured it out. I knew you would." He smiled, and then swept me up into a hug. Then he set me down and sent me a telepathic message.

It's time to go to CRANG.

Chapter 16:
Where You Go, I Go

My dad started waking up a little while later. He had been sleeping almost constantly since we brought him home from the hospital yesterday, only waking up to go to the bathroom and take a few sips of water. It had been two hours since my Crang discovery. I really wanted to get on the road and go find my mom and the others, but I couldn't leave without saying good bye to my daddy. I didn't want to think about it but, if things didn't go as planned, it might be the last time I saw him.

I didn't want to wake him, so I just sat at the edge of his bed watching him sleep, hoping I wouldn't have to wait too long.

I still found it hard to believe that my big strong daddy was lying practically helpless right in front of me. The man who had protected me all of my life. The man who made me dinner, tucked me in at night and even styled my hair for me until I learned the good sense to do it myself. Now I was the one taking care of him. But I couldn't even do that right. I was about to leave him ... maybe forever.

"How are you feeling, Daddy?" I asked when I saw his eyes start to flicker.

"Like I've been stabbed in the chest." My dad groaned and tried to sit up. "Seriously, though, I'm fine. I'll live. You and Josh really shouldn't have taken me to the hospital. It was risky."

"It was too risky to not take you, Dad. You could have died."

"You know how I feel about hospitals." My dad swung his feet over the side of the bed. He took a deep breath and tried to stand but lost his balance. I rushed to his side and caught him before he collapsed to the floor.

"Thanks, Priss," he said as he let me help him back to a sitting position.

"You should rest, Daddy. I'll get Josh to bring you something to eat. You need to keep your strength up."

He laid his head back and shut his eyes while taking deep breaths. He must have been in so much pain. Not only did he hate hospitals, he also hated pain medication, which meant he was coping with the pain all by himself. I felt really bad for him. I kind of wished he was part mutant like I was. When I broke into the Selliwood Institute to save the other specimens, I was shot and stabbed yet I was still able to fight. My wounds healed in just a few hours.

"Okay, I'll eat something," he said with his eyes still closed. "But first we need to pack a few things and move to a safer location. Give me a couple of hours and I should be strong enough to get on the road."

I sat back down at the edge of the bed and looked at my hands. "I knew you were going to say that, Daddy." I sighed and said, "I don't want to move. I'm tired of running and hiding. I can't do this anymore."

"Well, what do you propose we do, Priss? It's not safe here. I don't know what has happened to your mother. She could come back any minute and try to kill us all."

I took a deep breath. "I know. But if we run now, we'll be running for the rest of our lives. Colonel Selliwood needs to be stopped, and I'm going to stop him."

My father lifted his head and stared at me. He knew I was serious. And he also knew it would be very, no, incredibly hard to stop me, especially in his condition. So, he just asked, "What do you plan on doing? We don't know where to find him."

"I do. I know where he is. I figured it out."

He was silent.

I stood and zipped up my blue North Face jacket.

"I have to go, Daddy."

"Priss, wait." He tried to lean forward and grab my hand. He grimaced in pain then fell back down to the bed. "Think about this. I don't know what I'd do if I lost both you and your mother."

I saw tears build in his eyes. My big strong Daddy was reduced to tears at the thought of losing me or my mom. It broke my heart, but I had no choice.

"I have thought about it, Daddy. I have to do this. You're not going to lose me. I'm going to get my mother back. And I'm going to bring her home."

I kissed the top of his bald head then dashed out of the room before he could see the tears in my eyes as well.

When I came down the stairs, Josh, Marco, Ryan and Ian were standing by the front door. Josh had his arms crossed over a bullet proof vest. He had on one of Dad's gun harnesses which allowed him to carry three different weapons. Ryan and Marco had changed into what I had nicknamed "battle gear." Ryan's grey spandex suit was made out of a synthetic fiber that wouldn't disintegrate when he flew in different types of atmospheres. After our mission to United Arab Emirates, Dad had designed a suit for Marco with a built-in heating mechanism to keep him warm when he converted to metal. Ian wore the same jeans and button-down white shirt that he wore the night I met him. I wondered for a second if anyone would be able to design some clothes for him that could go with him through objects. For now, he just leaned against the door, tossing his cowboy hat into the air and catching it.

"What do you guys think you're doing?" I asked. Well, it was pretty obvious what they thought they were doing. They thought they were coming with me. I didn't need their help. I could do this alone. Well, with a little help from Tai. No one else knew it yet, but she was about to be my sidekick again.

"I know what you're planning, Priss. We're going with you," Marco said.

I shook my head. "I can do this on my own."

"She took my brother," Ryan said. "I don't care what you say. I'm going with you to get him back."

"She's my mother too, you know," Josh said. "And she's carrying my baby sister."

My eyes expanded. "It's a girl? How do you know it's a girl?" Josh gave me a 'duh' look. "Right, psychic. I forgot. What about that guy?" I asked, nodding toward Ian from New Zealand wondering why he needed to come.

"Katya is his sister. He's just as invested in this as we are. Besides, he can walk through walls. He could be very useful."

"Yeah, if we don't mind getting flashed." I rolled my eyes.

"Oh come on, sheila. You're just afraid to admit you might need me."

"I'm not afraid of anything." That was kind of a lie, but it sounded good at the time.

I took a step toward Marco, trying my best not to think of Ian any longer than I had to. "What about you? What's your reason for going?" I really didn't have to ask that. I could've looked into his intense eyes and known the answer.

He reached for my hand and said, "Where you go, I go."

Chapter 17:
Changing Channels

"Priss, where are you going? You're off course," Josh said, staring at the navigational system.

"We gotta make a quick detour."

Josh looked at me. "What? Why?"

"We have to get Tai."

"Who's Tai?" Ian asked.

"She's Priss' best friend," Josh volunteered. "But I really don't understand what she has to do with this mission."

"Oh no, you're not plannin' on goin' to get your nails done with your mate, are ya?" Ian said in his increasingly annoying accent.

"Sit down and shut up before I knock you back to Australia."

"Don't you start with me —"

"Guys, seriously. We don't have time for this," Josh interrupted. "Ian, if my sister says we need to get Tai, then we need to get Tai. This is her mission, so get used to it."

Tai was in Denmark getting ready to take some big important international science test, right? But it wasn't enough for her to fly halfway across the world just for a test; she also had to spend two weeks there in some sort of smart people camp. I knew at summer camp, kids sat around a campfire and tell stories. What did they do at science camp? Sit around a Bunsen burner and recite the periodic table? I shivered at the thought.

Thankfully, it was still dark when we arrived in Copenhagen. The cloaking device was working perfectly so we didn't get picked up on radar as we landed in an old airfield twenty miles outside the city.

Tai was waiting for me in front of her dorm room. "You okay, Prissy?" she said, giving me a hug.

I didn't realize how much I'd missed my best friend until I saw her again. I almost started crying, but that wasn't going to happen. Not in front of Ian anyway. He would've just made a smart remark about me being weak and girly.

So instead, I just took a deep breath and said, "I'm fine. I just want my mom back. What have you got for us?"

Tai looked both ways then started walking toward this big white dome-looking building. Once she got there, she pressed a code into the alarm system keypad on the door and then opened it. "This is the Chemistry lab," she said, walking in and flipping on the lights. "The lab used to be in the basement of the dormitory until last year's unfortunate bubble bath experiment. Don't ask." Tai sat down in front of a lab table. The two collars that my mom and Josh once wore lay on top. When she turned on a computer and started typing, one of the collars lit up.

"How'd you do that?" Ryan asked, taking a step back. He grabbed his neck terrified at the memory of what those things could do.

"Radio waves," Tai said simply.

"So how is all this supposed to work?" I asked, looking at the all too familiar inhibitor collars. Like Ryan, I didn't even want to get too close either. Though they would never admit it, Josh, Marco and Ian were afraid as well. Josh started sweating, Ian nervously twirled his hat and Marco started converting to metal. I had never worn one but I could imagine it had to be painful. Maybe not even physically. Our powers were a part of us; any device that took them away had to feel like losing yourself.

"Well, I remembered you telling me that the chips in the Specimens' brains were originally placed there to enhance the genetic mutations," Tai began. "Well, this device can neutralize those genetic mutations, right? The only way that would be possible is if they somehow blocked synapses in the brain through some sort of electrolysis or electromagnetic wavelength. So that got me thinking. The collars must use an electromagnetic currency or radio wave to the brain to inhibit the use of your genetic mutations. Well, the microchip is in the brain. Ergo, there should be a way to use the collar to communicate with the chip."

I blinked several times and shook my head. Did she really expect me to understand anything she just said?

"So, you've figured out a way to take over the microchip?" Josh asked.

"Not quite. That would take years," she said, pressing a few buttons on one of the collars.

"Well then why are we here if you don't know what you're doing?" arrogant Ian asked still twirling his cowboy hat. I gave him the evil eye hoping that would be enough to shut him up. It wasn't. "I knew we shouldn't have trusted the sheila. We could be in the Arctic Circle now saving my sister. We're wasting time."

"Wow. He *is* a jerk," Tai said, staring at Ian from New Zealand.

"Told you." I crossed my arms and leaned against another lab table.

"So, if you can't take over the microchip, what can you do?" Josh asked, ignoring Ian's remark.

"Two days ago, the first night we were here, some of the other engineering students and I snuck into the Chemistry kids' dorm rooms and rigged the radios and alarm clocks so that they only played one song." Tai started chuckling. "The next day, they were so confused when all of their radios would only play *She Blinded Me with Science*. It was hilarious." Tai was laughing so hard she actually slapped her knee.

We all just stared at her.

Marco leaned over to me and whispered, "Is this another human joke that I don't understand? Like the feces?"

I shook my head. "No, this isn't funny. It's just plain lame."

Tai cleared her throat and became serious again when she realized no one was laughing at her joke ... if you could call it that. "Anyway, that's when I got the idea of recalibrating the inhibitor. Priss told me that Josh's powers of hypnotic suggestion were kind of like tuning

139

into someone's thought wavelength and kind of changing the channel. So, what I did, or what I've tried to do, is turn the inhibitor into like a radio dial. I can change the channel."

"To what?" I asked.

Tai shrugged. "Not sure. But anything would be better than the channel they're on now, right? At least it should buy you enough time to overpower them."

"How can you be sure it'll work?" Josh asked.

"I can't. Which is why I'm gonna need a volunteer," Tai said, staring at us.

"I'll do it," I said. I mean she was my friend. I guess I should be the one to try out her contraption just in case anything went wrong.

Tai shook her head. "Actually, it can't be you or Josh. You don't have a microchip."

Right. That made sense.

Josh and I stared at Ryan, Marco, and Ian hoping one of them would volunteer. If not, what were we supposed to do, play eenie meenie miney moe?

"I'll do it," Marco said finally as he stepped forward.

"Thanks Marco," I said. I couldn't help it, but I got a little nervous when Marco volunteered. I knew it had to be hard for him. When I saved him from the Selliwood Institute, he and eleven other kids were locked in a room wearing those collars like powerless, trapped animals. I hated for him to be reminded of that.

Plus, what if something went wrong? I didn't want Marco to get hurt. Why couldn't Ian volunteer? I wouldn't mind him getting a little electrocuted or something.

"Okay, when I put this on you, not only will you not have your powers, but you're going to start thinking differently," Tai said as she stood on a chair so she'd be able to reach Marco's neck as well as press buttons on the top of the collar. "You ready?"

Marco nodded, but I don't think he was really ready. His entire torso was already metal and it was spreading. He was scared. As soon as Tai clicked on the inhibitor, the metal in his body vanished.

"How do you feel?" Tai asked.

"Gotta say. I've never felt better," he said in perfect American English. His French accent was completely gone.

A weird smile crept over Marco's face. I mean, it was a gorgeous smile. It was just weird because I had never seen him smile so big before. And he had this mischievous sparkle in his eyes. He took a step toward me and for some reason, my heart started beating rapidly. What in the world was he up to? Oh no, what if Tai had changed the channel to a crazy station? What if he was about to kill me or something?

Marco stopped walking and stood like an inch in front of me. He still had this huge grin on his face. Out of the corner of my eye, I saw Josh lunge toward Marco. Apparently, he was concerned about Marco's strange behavior as well.

"No worries, mate. No worries," Ian said, holding Josh back.

Suddenly Marco grabbed my hand and spun me around and started swaying from side to side. Wait a minute, he wasn't swaying. He was dancing. Marco was dancing? That was *so* not like him.

"*I never knew the charm of Spring. Never made it face to face. I never knew my heart could sing. Never missed a warm embrace*," Marco sang while dancing me around the lab. He sounded like he should be wearing a velvet jacket and singing in a lounge somewhere in Vegas.

"What is he doing?" I asked over my shoulder.

"Singing," smart alec Ian provided.

"Well I know that. But why? Does he think he's Michael Bublé?"

"He's actually singing *April in Paris*. It's a Sinatra classic," Ian added.

I rolled my eyes. "Tai? What's going on?" I asked as I tried to follow along with Marco's dance moves. I didn't know when he'd learned to ballroom dance but he was actually pretty good. I just had to match his feet and try not to get dizzy.

"He's not himself," Tai answered as she followed us around the room. She tried to poke her head in between us several times trying to study him. His eyes seemed different. They were still the same amazing green color, but they seemed a little far away.

Suddenly, we stopped moving. Then Marco tipped me back and planted a kiss on my lips. At first, I was really tense because I thought the nausea would hit any second. But then as the kiss kept going and there were no signs of puking, I actually started to enjoy the kiss.

Finally, he let me up for air and said, "Now that I can get used to."

Breathing heavily I studied my hands and legs. No metal. I had finally kissed Marco without vomit or turning into a statue. It was a dream come true. Just when I was about to go in for round two, Tai reached up and clicked off the collar.

"What happened?" Marco asked, shaking his head like a puppy coming out of a pool.

"You just played tonsil tennis with ya sheila there," Ian said. "And you pranced around the room like some sort of ballerina."

"I did? In front of everyone?" Poor Marco was so embarrassed. He jammed his hands into his pockets and looked away from me.

"Yeah, and it was gross," Ryan added.

Marco started blushing. OMG he was so cute! I still hadn't caught my breath back from the kiss and the red tinge in his super tanned cheeks made it even harder to breathe.

"I can't believe I did that. That is not like me at all."

"Exactly," Tai said confidently as she slipped the collar off of Marco's neck. "I think it's ready."

Chapter 18:
Meant to Be

"Well, as fascinating as that was, we better be on our way now," Ian said, snatching the collars away from Tai.

She gave him a fierce look then quickly went back to her normally sweet self. "Great. Just let me pack up a few things," Tai said, reaching for a laptop on a table behind her.

"Where do you think you're going?" Ian asked.

"What do you mean? I have to go, too. I have to. No one else knows how to work these." She snatched the collars back from Ian then waved them in the air.

I was so proud of her for standing up to Ian. I couldn't help but smile. No longer was she the shy little girl who let eighth graders bully her out of ice cream that was rightfully hers or uninvite her to a dance. Somewhere along the way she had developed some confidence and,well, a backbone. I wondered if Spencer had something to do with that. Or maybe she just finally realized how awesome she was.

"She's right you know," I said, standing next to my best friend and crossing my arms. "What if something goes wrong and she needs to make a last second adjustment? None of us would have any idea what to do."

"This is ridiculous. This whole mission is turning into some sort of sheila slumber party." Ian threw his hat in the air in frustration then stormed out of the building. Ryan caught the hat in mid air then flew out right behind Ian.

Marco looked back and forth between me and where Ian and Ryan had gone. I could tell he was still embarrassed about kissing me and dancing in front of everyone the way he kept putting his hands in his pockets then yanking them out every two seconds. Finally, he took off toward the door.

Josh sighed. "Tai," he said, turning to her. He grabbed both her shoulders and stared directly into her eyes. "I know you want to help us and I appreciate all that you've already done. But this is going to be extremely dangerous. We can't guarantee your safety."

Tai nodded. "I ... I ... I know what I'm getting into. I also know that you and Priss need me. I want to do this. I wanna come."

Josh started shaking his head.

"It's my mission," I said, stepping in between him and Tai. "You said so yourself. My mission, my decision. She's coming."

"Fine, but she's your responsibility." Josh turned and went after the other boys.

"You sure you want to do this?" I asked her once Josh had left.

Tai didn't even acknowledge me. She just kept staring after Josh. "Holy hot chocolate. He's so beautiful," she said in almost a whisper.

I rolled my eyes. She really needed to get over this crush on my brother she obviously had.

"Tai, snap out of it!" I said, snapping my fingers next to her ears. "I asked you a question."

"Oh, what?" She turned to me and blinked rapidly as if she was coming out of a trance.

"I said, are you sure you want to do this?"

"I can't believe you would even ask me that," she said with a 'duh' look on her face. "You're my best friend. You risked your life to save mine. And I know you would do it again in a heartbeat. This is the least I can do."

Without Ian around to pick on me, I let a few tears escape. She hugged me and said, "We're gonna get your mom back." Tai smiled and then went back to packing up her computer, the collars, and a bunch of wires.

"By the way, I was wrong," she said after a few minutes.

"About what?" I hopped up on a lab table while wiping away the last of my tears.

"About Marco. I think maybe you two are meant to be together."

"Why?"

"When I changed his channel, the first thing he did was take you in his arms like some old classic movie and kiss you."

"So?"

Tai stopped packing for a second and looked at me. "There are an infinite number of personalities he could have assumed. The chances that he chose one where he was still in love with you is miniscule."

"So what does that mean?"

"It means you are deeply hotwired into his brain, girl. It's like you're a part of him no matter what channel his brain is on."

I thought about that for a second. It made complete sense. It would explain why I'd always felt so connected to him. What did that mean for us?

"As long as he's wearing a collar, you won't have to worry about the side effects of a metal conversion," she added. "You might actually be able to have a normal relationship. Well, normal for you anyway."

"Thanks a lot," I said, balling up a piece of paper and tossing it at her head.

"Hey watch it or I'll ... I'll ... " Tai had no imagination when it came to comebacks. "I'll program him to miss your birthday every year." Tai smiled as if that was funny or clever or something. How lame. I rolled my eyes.

"What about Kyle?" I asked

Tai shrugged. "Maybe you can be friends again. I still think you need each other. But we're only thirteen. It's not like you have to sign your marriage license or something. Who knows what the future holds?"

She had a point. There was no telling what would happen between Kyle and me in the future. Hey, there was no telling what would happen tonight. I might not even survive this mission. If I did, I'd have plenty of time to worry about my relationship drama later. I just didn't see how it would be possible to tell Kyle the truth one day and have a "normal" relationship with him. I sighed and tried to shake the thought from my mind. I really needed to focus on my mission.

"You almost ready?" I asked, jumping off the table.

Tai stuffed a few more things into her backpack, zipped it up and said, "Okay, I'm ready. Let's do this."

Chapter 19:
Tracked

We were flying toward the Arctic Circle for what felt like a year before any of us came up with a plan. It was probably more like ten minutes but with the angry silence that filled the jet, it felt so much longer. Well, I guess the guys could have had a plan, but if they did, they weren't sharing. I think they were still kind of mad at me for bringing Tai along. I had no choice though. She was the only one who could work the collars. I glanced over at her in the copilot's seat typing away at her laptop, which she somehow connected to the jet's console. I sure hoped she knew what she was doing.

I hadn't really put too much thought into what I would do once I got to the North Pole. Part of me was hoping I would just be able to walk into whatever camp or building Selliwood had built, toss my mother over my shoulder and walk out. I knew it would be ridiculously more complicated than that. I mean, first of all, I didn't even know where exactly they were. I mean, the arctic was a big place.

"Look," I said finally. "I know you're all mad at me or whatever but that's not going to get us anywhere." I craned my head back and made sure my voice projected to the back of the jet so that they could hear me. "We're gonna have to work together."

No one said anything or even acknowledged that I was talking. I started going through all the inspirational movies I'd seen lately and trying to think of the best pep talk to steal when Josh stood up and joined me in the cock pit. Marco was a couple of steps behind. Good thing. I didn't think my *Remember the Titans* speech applied to the current situation.

I still wasn't sure what we were going to do, but working together was a good first step. Thankfully, I was flying with the smartest people I knew. I was sure one of them would be able to figure something out. Tai started tinkering with the radar system making adjustments so she could pick up the slightest signs of Selliwood and company. Josh and Marco stood between Tai and me and used the computer system on the jet to find out anything they could about the arctic. Ian sulked in the back with his hat over his face. Ryan stared out of the window either looking for clues or enjoying the view. I couldn't really figure out which.

"There's an abandoned helicopter landing pad that was used during a Soviet expedition through the Arctic about twelve years ago," Marco said, standing between Josh and me in the front seats of the cockpit. "I bet that's where he lands his aircrafts before going to their actual station."

"We should be able to land there, then head to Selliwood's exact location on foot. He can't be too far," Josh said.

"How do you know? What if he just lands directly on the ice and he's nowhere near this location?" I asked.

Marco shook his head. "Let's hope not. Landing on ice might be fine for a helicopter, but the jet is too heavy. I wouldn't risk it. According to what we're reading here," he said, pointing to the screen, "the thickness of the sea ice has been decreasing over the past several years. Global Warming. I don't want us to end up sinking."

I stole a glance at Marco. I couldn't help but get a little nervous for him. If something happened and he fell through the ice as metal, he'd sink to the bottom and freeze to death.

***

"There's nothing out here, Priss," Tai said with a sigh. "I've got the radar to a range of over 500 miles in any direction. I got nothing. Maybe you were wrong."

"I can't be wrong," I said as we circled the Arctic Circle for the third time. This was our only lead, our only hope. But so far, we hadn't seen buildings, or construction, or any evidence that Colonel Selliwood

156

had built some kind of base. My heart sank. Maybe we'd never find my mother.

"What are we gonna do? What if we can't find them?" I said, trying to swallow my panic. Now was not the time to flip out. Finding my mother and the others was too important.

We all stared out into the blanket of white outside the jet in silence. A huge polar bear sat on the edge of the ice staring into the water. Seconds later, a fish jumped up out of the water. The polar bear jumped in the air and caught the fish in its mouth before splashing into the water.

"Did you see that?" Ryan said excitedly. "He was like a dog going after a Frisbee!"

"Uh huh, yeah," I grumbled. I really wasn't interested in the *National Geographic* spectacle taking place outside. Not when we had a mission to accomplish. Apparently, Josh and Marco weren't in the mood to observe the scenery either. They didn't even look away from the computer monitor. Tai, on the other hand, stopped what she was doing and looked up. She

157

hopped out of her seat and joined Ryan in the back as he looked out of the window.

"And then he just jumped into the water," Ryan continued as if it was the coolest thing he had ever seen.

"Hey, guys," Tai said in a weird kind of tone. She sounded like a cross between scared and curious. Let's call it scarious. "What if the base is underground ... or underwater?"

We looked at each other. Then we all looked out of the window. Why didn't I think of that?

"That's extremely possible," Marco said. "Colonel Selliwood wouldn't want to build something that was easily found. He'd want as much secrecy as possible."

"You see! Aren't you happy I brought her? Good job, Tai!" I held up my hand for a high five and she crossed back into the cockpit to give me one.

"Good job my arse. How exactly are we supposed to find an underwater base, and once we find it, how are we supposed to get in?" Ian said, entering the cockpit. It was starting to get really crowded in there.

"I don't think we have to worry about finding them," Josh said as he stared straight ahead with a look of dread on his face. "I think they just found us."

I looked down at the radar and noticed two aircrafts following us.

Ian came over and stared at the screen as well. Then he closed his eyes. "One of them is Katya," he said.

"How do you know?" Tai asked.

"I know my sister. It's a twin thing."

"The other one is Peter," Ryan added. "I can feel it."

"How did they find us?" I said, preparing for evasive maneuvers. "I know Dad and Will Smith fixed the cloaking mechanism."

The next time I looked at Marco, he had turned completely to metal. "Maybe they are not tracking the jet. Maybe they are tracking us. Me, Ryan and Ian. Maybe the micro chip in our brains sends off a signal that can be picked up on within a certain range."

I looked at Josh. He shrugged. "I guess that's possible."

"Buckle up, boys," I said, pulling the jet into a hard left.

Marco fell backwards and landed on his metal butt. Ryan flew to his seat and quickly put on his belt.

"Think about it," Marco said after getting his bearings and buckling into his seat. "Each time the jet was tracked, you were with one of us."

"You're right," I said. "In UAE I was with you and during the air fight over the Gulf of Mexico I was with Katya." I swung the jet upside down so that I was flying on top of the planes that were tailing us. I noticed Ryan turn a shade of green. How could he get sick during a flight? He could fly. "So how do you suppose we get out of this?"

Marco looked at Ryan. "How strong do you feel?"

Ryan knew exactly what Marco was suggesting. "I guess I have to be strong enough to carry the two of you," he said, indicating Marco and Ian.

"We'll meet up with you later," Marco said unbuckling his belt and standing. He headed for the door. "We'll try to get them off your tail. Maybe they'll follow us and leave you alone."

"Marco don't! That's suicide," I said. I started to panic. He was about to kill himself just to save me. Of course, Ian was going too. I didn't really care about Ian. He could leap out of the plane now for all I cared. Not Marco though. He meant too much to me. I couldn't let him do it. I would've jumped up and tried to slap some sense into him, but I had to fly the jet.

"Josh, take the controls," I said, hopping out of my seat and letting Josh take over. I wrapped my arms around Marco. "Don't. Please don't," I whispered into his metal chest.

"She's right," Josh said. "There are two of them. They could easily split up and come after both us."

"Well, I don't see you coming up with any other ideas," Ian said. "What are we supposed to do?"

"I don't think it matters anymore, guys," Josh said, taking his hands off the controls. "They've taken over the jet."

Chapter 20:
The Loading Dock

I took Tai's usual seat at the copilot's position just to make sure. We had lost complete control of the jet. No matter what buttons I pressed or how hard I pulled up, we kept being dragged slowly toward the white sheet of ice beneath us. It was like being pulled by a giant magnet or tractor beam.

"Priss, do something!" Josh yelled.

"I'm trying. Nothing's working!" I kept banging away at the console. "There's nothing I can do." I finally gave up and put my head in my hands. I had to hold back tears. I felt kind of like what I imagined a pig headed to the slaughterhouse would feel. I was sure we'd be dead. This was all my fault. This was my mission and I'd failed.

How in the world could we get out of this? I was praying for a miracle.

"Hello, Priscilla." Colonel Selliwood's face popped up on the holophone and I jumped. "We've been expecting you," he continued. Ian lunged for the image as if he could actually punch Colonel Selliwood. Marco grabbed him and held him back.

If Marco was afraid, he sure didn't show it. His shiny metal face showed nothing but confidence and determination. I wondered if he had a plan.

Ryan and Ian's emotions were a bit easier to see. They wanted to rip Colonel Selliwood's head off right there. Even though he was only eight years old, I'm sure Ryan was trained enough to kill Colonel Selliwood in a matter of minutes. He was literally shaking with anger. Josh stood up and put a hand on Ryan's shoulder to calm him. I wondered if he had sent him a telepathic message as well. When he looked at Josh and nodded, I knew they were communicating.

"Things are going to go a bit differently than the last time we met, Priscilla," Colonel Selliwood said. "When we land your jet, just come out peacefully." Colonel Selliwood's holographic face peered around the cockpit. "And what do we have here? Specimen Iota. It's been a long time. Did you ever work out your nudity issues?"

For the first time since I'd met him, Ian was stunned silent. I actually felt kind of bad for him. Selliwood's taunting had to be humiliating.

"Nothing to say?" Colonel Selliwood continued. "I can see the reprogramming is going to take a bit of work on you. You've been gone too long. But, hey, if it worked on Specimen Q it can work on anyone."

"Specimen Mu and Specimen Rho," he said, talking to Marco and Ryan. "Welcome back. Don't try anything stupid and I might let the little Sumners live."

I noticed Marco flinch at that statement. Marco was not about to let Colonel Selliwood take me without a fight. I could see it in his eyes.

"Priscilla," Ian said once the holophone clicked off. "I know this is your mission and I'm sure you have a plan. But I think I speak for all of us when I say if anything goes wrong, just light this place up. I don't care if we're inside or not. I'd rather be dead than under that man's control."

Ryan nodded in agreement.

I looked at Marco hoping he'd be the voice of reason. I wanted him to say that nothing was gonna go wrong and we were all going to get out safely, but instead he said, "I agree with Ian. I would rather be dead."

"No one's dying," I said. "We're gonna get out of this together. Right, Josh?" I looked at my brother, but he turned away from me. I thought he had tears in his eyes. He knew something. He knew one or all of us weren't going to make it.

"Josh, if you —"

"Priss, I found something," Tai said interrupting me. She was oddly calm. Normally, at this amount of danger, Tai would be curled up in the fetal position rubbing her

165

rock collection. I hadn't even noticed that she was still tinkering with the computer. If we made it out of here alive, she was definitely getting promoted from best friend to ... I don't know. What was higher than best friend? I guess a sister. Tai would forever be my sister. Maybe we could even get matching outfits.

"What?" I asked, leaning over her shoulder.

"It's a blueprint of the underwater base. See that there?" she said, pointing to the screen. "There's a ridiculous amount of radio waves coming from that room. I think that's where I need to be."

Just then, we landed with a thud on the ice. Glass walls rose from the ground and covered us so that it felt like we were in a giant snow globe. Then the ground gave way slowly, dropping us into the Earth.

I looked out of the window of the jet and noticed that we were being lowered into what looked like a loading zone of some sort. And we weren't alone. Besides Katya and Peter, there were at least twelve armed guards waiting for us at the bottom.

"Okay, here's what we're gonna do," I said with as much confidence as I could fake. "Josh, you take Tai to this room she's talking about."

"What about Katya? I want to save her," he protested.

"I thought you said this was my mission? I know what I'm doing!" I lied. I had no idea what I was doing. "Tai is going to need your protection."

"She's right, Josh. Don't worry. I'll get Katya," Ian said.

Whoa. Wait. What? Did Ian just agree with me?

"Ian and Ryan," I said trying to not show my shock. "You guys take care of Peter, and Katya. Use the collars that Tai modified."

"What about you? What are you going to use for Mom?" Josh asked.

I shrugged. I hadn't thought that far in advance. All I knew was that we were not going to get out of that loading dock with Peter and Katya there. We only had two modified collars. We had to use them now.

167

"I don't know. I'll figure something out," I said and then I turned toward Marco, "You're with me."

He nodded his metal head and crossed his arms over his chest.

Suddenly, we stopped moving. I glanced out the window and saw Peter and Katya standing with guns trained on the door of our jet. I had never seen either of them use a firearm before. As far as I knew, all of the specimens preferred to use their own abilities and training in battle. They felt since they already had so many genetic advancements, using a gun was just plain unfair. I had to remember that Peter and Katya weren't really Peter and Katya anymore.

Hands shaking, Tai was making some final adjustments to the collars before handing them over to Ian. I sure hoped those things worked.

Marco ran out of the jet first, skillfully deflecting all the bullets shot from Peter and Katya. Ian followed and stayed close by Marco until he could find a good opening to go after Katya. He found it when Katya looked down for a split second in order to reload her weapon.

Another reason why specimens never used guns. You were always vulnerable when you had to reload.

Ian ran and tackled his sister, knocking the gun out her hands. They rolled around the ground for a second until Katya kicked him off. She rolled over and went to stomp on his neck, but Ian grabbed her foot and twisted it making her land face down in the concrete.

Josh closed his eyes and turned his head. "It's gonna be okay, Josh. Ian's not gonna hurt his sister," I said.

I nearly missed Ryan flying out into the action, but he went next and headed straight for Peter who was hovering near a light fixture and firing at Marco. As soon as Ryan was close enough, he kicked the gun away. Peter responded by punching Ryan in the face sending him into a backward spiral through the air. Ryan and Ian were in for a long fight.

As Tai cowered behind me, I surveyed the room. Several jets and helicopters in various colors and sizes lined one side of the room. On the other side, there was a glass room with computers and a bunch of high tech gadgets.

"You ready, Tai?" Josh asked as he clicked the safety off one of his guns.

"I-I-I-" she stuttered. She was totally freaked. The calm confidence she had just a few minutes ago when she was in front of her computer had all but disappeared.

"Don't worry, Tai. I won't let anything happen to you." Josh tried to reassure her and even wrapped his arm around her for a second. "Which way do we need to go?"

Tai pointed a shaky finger to a door on the left.

"All right, let's do it," he said.

I turned and gave Tai a big hug. "Take care of my best friend," I told Josh.

"She'll be fine," he said, looking directly into my eyes. Then he looked out into the loading zone and sighed. I knew what that meant. Someone out there wasn't going to make it.

Josh jumped out of the jet, staying low in case more gun fire came. Tai was practically glued to his side.

I decided to dash for a door in the opposite direction that said *Exit*. I hoped it led to the rest of the compound and not to the freezing waters of the Arctic Ocean. I should have taken a few more minutes to study the blueprints Tai found. I really had no idea where I was going.

I leapt out of the jet and made a run for it. I blasted a hole through the door and jumped through it headfirst. I didn't land in the ocean. It was a corridor. I got to my feet just in time to get knocked over by Marco who had jumped through right behind me.

"You weren't trying to leave me behind were you?" he said, getting to his feet and helping me up. "I told you before, where you go, I go."

Chapter 21:
The Elephant on the Broom

What was I thinking? I thought as Marco and I slinked along walls and poked our heads into room after room. Clearly, I wasn't thinking. That was the only explanation for how I could end up alone with Marco. Maybe I did it on purpose. Maybe I just wanted to spend time with him. No, that wasn't it. He and I together was just logical. It only made sense that Ian and Ryan fought their own twins. They'd match each other in skill level. And Tai certainly couldn't be left on her own. But I guess I could have sent Marco with her and Josh with me. I shook my head. Whatever the case, I couldn't change my mind now and the tension between us was making it hard for me to concentrate. Every time he even accidentally brushed his metal body against mine, sparks flew. Not literally ... this time anyway.

The narrow steel hallways reminded me of a submarine. Old timey light bulbs hung from the ceiling. This place definitely wasn't as high tech as the Selliwood Institute was. I wondered if Colonel Selliwood was having financial trouble. Who cared? Why was I thinking about that? I shook my head and tried to focus.

"So when are we going to talk about the elephant on the broom?" Marco asked as we checked out yet another empty room.

I stopped and stared at him. I shook my head a couple of times trying to clear out the cobwebs or whatever was taking up so much space in my head that I was now hearing things. Elephants and brooms? Did I hear him right? "What are you talking about?" I asked.

"You know. The elephant on the broom. It is an American saying, no?"

I stared at him some more while squinting my eyes in confusion. Had Tai's little collar trick given him brain damage?

"You know. Me and you. The elephant," he continued.

"Oh!" I said finally understanding what he was trying to say. "First of all, the saying is *the elephant in the room*. Although, if there was an elephant on a broom, we'd definitely need to talk about that, too. Second of all, we're on a mission. I think we should concentrate on finding my mom and then getting out of here. Later maybe we can talk about ... other things."

Marco nodded. "Of course, you are right. We should focus."

We took a few steps in silence. Suddenly, he said, "It's just that with what Tai has done to the collars, it opens up so many more ... opportunities for us. I was able to kiss you without any dangerous side effects."

"Yes, but you also didn't remember it. You weren't yourself when you had that collar on."

"True, but I'm sure Tai can make some further adjustments and make it work more efficiently for our purposes."

I stopped again. "Our purposes? What exactly are our purposes?" I asked with a grin. I knew exactly what he was talking about. I just wanted to see him squirm. He was even cuter when he was nervous.

"Um," he said, averting his eyes

I decided to let him off the hook. "And you'd be willing to wear that collar again just to be with me?"

He nodded. "I'd do anything for you."

I think my insides melted on the spot. What are you supposed to do when a ridiculously cute boy says something like that to you?

We stared at each other for a moment that could have lasted forever. Unfortunately, our special moment was interrupted by my super hearing. I heard a gun engage and then a bullet slice through the air. It bounced off of Marco's shoulder and grazed my cheek.

Marco knocked me to the ground and blocked the other bullets with his body. "Oh my, no! You're hit!

You're hit!" he said, wiping the blood from my face with his metal fingers. He was actually scratching me more than the bullet did.

"I'm fine," I said, trying to look past Marco and see who was shooting. "It barely touched me."

I pushed Marco out of the way a little and got a good look at none other than Specimen Xi. I rolled my eyes. I really didn't feel like dealing with Xi. She was annoyingly hard to defeat. She had no pain receptors, which meant she never even felt it when I burned her and she could grow back skin and body parts. The last time we fought her in the United Arab Emirates, Marco and I had to cut off both her hands in order to get away.

When the shooting stopped, Marco turned around and saw her as well. He grumbled something in French. He was annoyed too. Then he said, "We don't want any problems, Xi. We just want Mrs. Sumner back."

Xi didn't respond. That wasn't like her. Usually she would have said some rude remark or at least insulted my outfit by now. I stared into her eyes. She didn't look the same. She looked ... stupid. Xi was a lot of things, but she wasn't dumb.

"I don't think that's Xi," I whispered to Marco.

"What? What do you mean?"

I sent a flame down the corridor and melted the gun in her hand. She yelped in pain. "See," I said. Specimen Xi would have laughed at the gun melting in her hand. She wouldn't have felt a thing.

"Specimen Zero," Marco said through clenched teeth. He hated the shape shifting Zero as much as I hated Xi. Well, almost as much. I don't think it was possible for anyone to hate someone as much as I hated that girl.

Two months ago, Specimen Zero posed as me and then kidnapped the President's daughter, Elizabeth Gonzalez. He (or it, we still weren't quite sure what it was) almost got me killed. Tai ended up having to shoot both of us because she couldn't tell us apart. I knew the bullet wouldn't hurt me, though, because Marco had just transferred his powers to me through, well, a kiss.

Before our eyes, Specimen Zero kind of melted back into his natural state. He looked really gross. Kind of like a skinny Hunchback of Notre Dame with transparent skin. Suddenly, he seemed to realize he was outnumbered and without a weapon. Specimen Zero turned and started running.

"We can't let him get away this time," I said. "Maybe he can lead us to Colonel Selliwood."

"Let's follow him," Marco said.

"You follow him. I'm gonna keep looking for my mother."

Marco looked concerned. "I don't think we should separate. Especially since you are injured."

"I'm not injured. I'm fine. The bullet barely touched me. You go after Zero, I'll go after my mother, and we'll meet in the loading dock in fifteen minutes."

He sighed and stared into my eyes, still unsure. I didn't quite know what else to say. I really didn't want to say anything. I just wanted to kiss him. "Fifteen minutes, Marco. You better be there," I said, grabbing the collar of his suit. "If you die, I'll kill you." Okay, so that made absolutely no sense but he got the point. He stared into my eyes with a smile then took off after Zero.

As Zero and Marco disappeared from sight, I tuned my super hearing and tried to listen for Zero's partner in crime. Zero was usually never too far away from Xi. I needed to be prepared for that psycho chick. But instead of hearing Xi's high heels and distinctive British accent, I heard something completely different and, well ... bizarre.

Chapter 22:
Big Willie's Back

Singing. I heard singing. Who in the world could possibly be singing in the underwater coffin we were in? I had no idea. And I wasn't close enough to even make out the words of the song. I know I had super hearing but something about being underwater must have affected how far sound carried. I stood up and followed the sound.

As I walked, I stared at the old timey light bulbs again. Suddenly, they started flickering. And then darkness.

Snap. Now how was I supposed to figure out where I was going? Wait a minute. What was I talking about? I was a human torch. I held up my hand and lit a flame. Hmph. That worked.

I kept walking, sliding along the cold walls trying to listen for ... Okay, I didn't know what I was listening for. All I knew was that someone was singing and that I had a feeling I needed to find that person. Although chances were pretty good that it was a psycho specimen, I refused to give up hope.

Suddenly, the lights flickered back on. That was a good sign, right? I shook my hand to extinguish the flame.

I focused my super hearing again and was finally able to make out the words of the song.

In West Philadelphia born and raised

On the play ground is where I spent most of my days

Chillin out maxin relaxin all cool

I was shootin some B-Ball outside of the school

When a couple of guys they was up to no good

Started causing trouble in my neighborhood

I got in one little fight and my mom got scared

She said 'You're movin' with your auntie and uncle in Bel Air'

I recognized that song from a show on Nick-at-Nite. It was the theme song to the *Fresh Prince of Bel-Air*. Specimen W! He was here! And judging from his choice of song, he was still himself and not taken over by Selliwood.

Specimen W was the first specimen my mother ever helped escape from the Selliwood Institute. It was twelve years ago when W was only sixteen-years-old. After being locked in the institute all of his life and only let out to kill someone occasionally, he was completely socially awkward. Think Marco times ten. He had never even seen a movie. After watching *Men in Black,* he became obsessed with Will Smith and even preferred to be called that which was pretty odd for a six foot white guy with a German accent.

I whistled for a cab and when it came near

The license plate said fresh and it had dice in the mirror

If anything I can say is that this cab was rare

But I thought 'Man forget it' — 'Yo home to Bel Air'

I noticed a hint of nervousness in his voice. He didn't have the normal enthusiasm he did whenever he sang a Will Smith song. He must have been singing in order to keep himself calm. There was no telling what he had already been through.

I followed the sound of his voice and found him strapped to a table in a lab room.

"Will Smith!" I yelled, wrapping my arms around him as best as I could. I mean he was lying on a table.

"Priscilla? What are you doing here?" He tried to sit up, but he was held firmly in place with metal straps.

"I came to save my mom and the others," I said while I went to loosen his restraints. Nothing I tried worked. I was super strong, but I couldn't pull those metal bands off without tearing into his skin and breaking his wrists. There had to be a better way to get him loose. I stared at my fingers. Melting could work. "Brace yourself, Will Smith. This is going to hurt a little." I stood back and melted the restraints two at a time. I could tell he wanted to scream, but he held it in.

"Your mother is being controlled by Colonel Selliwood," Will Smith said when I had finished. He tried to rub the pain out of the burn marks on his wrists.

"I know. They activated the microchip in her head."

"They have control over Peter and Katya as well," he said, hopping off the table and searching around the room. He must have been looking for his stick. When going into a fight, Will Smith always carried a long wooden stick, similar to the double light saber carried by Darth Maul in *Star Wars: The Phantom Menace* or like Gambit in X-Men. It was also just like the stick used by Specimen Gamma. I had defeated her the same night I rescued my parents from the Selliwood Institute.

"Yeah, I know that, too. We came to save them. Ryan and Ian are fighting Peter and Katya in the loading dock. Josh and Tai are trying to disrupt the signal. And Marco went after Specimen Zero."

"Ian is here? From New Zealand?"

I nodded. "Yeah, he came when he lost contact with his sister," I said, bending and looking under the table for W's stick.

"Where's your dad?" he asked.

"At home," I swallowed hard, holding back my emotion as I thought about my dad at home with his stab wounds. "My mom stabbed him and tried to kill him. I know she didn't mean to. It was Selliwood. He made her do it. Why didn't he take you over as well?" I asked, trying to change the subject a little.

"Every time Dr. Witherall comes near me with the device to activate my chip, I surge the electricity. I don't know how many days I've been here. They captured me the same night your mother attacked us, but they haven't figured out a way around the surging yet. They can't put an inhibitor on me because then the microchip won't work properly."

"I know. Tai figured out a way to modify the collars to counteract the effect of the microchip or something. Hopefully, Ian and Ryan are using them on Peter and Katya right now.

Will Smith found his stick locked away in a cabinet. As he strapped it to his back I asked, "Do you know where Colonel Selliwood and Dr. Witherall are?"

"We're right here," a sickeningly familiar voice said. It was Colonel Selliwood.

The wall behind us dissolved. It was just a hologram and on the other side of it was what looked like an observation room or an office. There were seats for people to watch what took place in the lab room where we were but there was also a desk, a computer and a couple of file cabinets. In the center of the room stood Colonel Selliwood, Dr. Witherall, and ... someone who used to be my mother.

Chapter 23:
Family Ties

Colonel Selliwood stood in front of me in a black military uniform with silver buttons almost as shiny as his silver hair. Witherall had on a white lab coat that really stood out against his dyed black hair. He still had that weird looking glass eye. What was up with that? They could create a shape shifting human like thingamajig, but they couldn't figure out a way to make his eye look normal.

My mother's appearance scared me more than Selliwood and Witherall combined. In her knee-length black leather jacket and matching leather pants, she looked like a character out of *The Matrix,* only deadlier. Her fiery red hair was wrapped in a tight bun. Her face was pale and stiff as stone. I thought she would be able to kill me with one look. But she didn't look at me. She didn't even acknowledge my existence. Wasn't there some sort of motherly bond that tied a mother to her daughter? Part of me wanted her to look into my eyes and see her baby girl and have that motherly instinct override Selliwood's programming. But that didn't happen. She just focused straight ahead with an expressionless and blinkless (is that a word?) stare.

"Little girl, I told you before you can't beat me," Colonel Selliwood said, walking toward me.

Specimen W whipped out his stick and braced himself for a fight.

"Q, handle him," Selliwood said simply.

My mother flipped into action. W tried to fend her off with his stick, but my mother split it in half with one swift swipe of her hand. W hesitated. He knew my mother was pregnant and he probably didn't want to hit her. His hesitation gave my mother enough time to kick the side of his head, which sent him reeling to the far wall of the room. I screamed. "Mom, don't!"

"She's not your mother anymore," Selliwood said with a creepy grin and a chuckle that made me want to knock his teeth in.

He was right though. That monstrous killing machine standing next to him was not my mother.

Dr. Witherall stood on the other side of her, making my mother the cream of some weird little evil sandwich cookie or something. I looked into Dr. Witherall's eyes and thought back to that necklace he gave me. I still couldn't figure out what his angle was. He was either trying to kill me or buying me expensive gifts. It was a twisted "He Loves Me, He Loves Me Not" game.

Dr. Witherall broke our eye lock first and I went back to staring at the person who looked like my mother.

"You might have control of her now, but I'm gonna get her back. And then I'm taking you down," I said with fake confidence.

Selliwood rolled his eyes. "Are we really going to have to go through this whole thing again? This isn't like the Institute hidden in the side of a mountain just waiting to be blown up. We are three hundred feet under freezing water. How do you think you're going to get out of here? You're trapped."

I opened my mouth to dispute him, but I couldn't. He was right. I had no escape plan. I couldn't very well swim to the surface. Even though I was technically a never ending source of fire, I'd still probably freeze to death after more than five minutes.

"Do you know why I chose the Arctic Circle for my little project, by the way?" he said, taking a cloth out of his pocket and buffing his buttons.

I shrugged. "I don't know. You have a thing for penguins?"

"Penguins are at the South Pole, not the North Pole." He sighed and rolled his eyes again. "What are they teaching you people in school these days?" He finished shining his buttons and put the cloth back in his pocket. "Anyway, the magnetic charge of the north pole is the perfect transmitter for the signal."

"What signal?"

"Mirror!" He commanded with a snap of his finger. My mother immediately pulled a compact out of her jacket pocket and handed it to him.

"The signal," he said as he used the mirror to check the shininess of his buttons, "that will activate all of the microchips in all of my specimens around the world. You know all those precious little assassins you kidnapped from me six months ago?" he asked, closing the compact and returning it to my mother. "Well soon, they'll be mine again. You see how nicely the reprogramming worked." He reached out and stroked my mother's hair like she was some sort of pet.

"Why can't you just leave us alone? All we want is to be a family. Do you know she's pregnant with my little sister?"

"Pregnant?" Dr. Witherall asked, speaking up for the first time. He had a look of ... a look of ...Well, I couldn't quite read his expression, but it looked a little like fear.

Now it was Colonel Selliwood's turn to shrug as he continued to pet my mother's head and stare into her face like she was a new toy that belonged to only him. "What do I care if she's pregnant?" He paused for a moment. "Actually, that does give me an idea for an experiment. Martin, why don't we see if we can extract the fetus? We can use the stem cells to improve Zero's mental development. We still don't know why that idiot can't talk."

I stared at him with my mouth open. How could he even think of something like that? My stomach turned at the thought.

My mother apparently didn't hear what he'd said in reference to her unborn child. She just stared in front of her blankly. She didn't recognize anything or anyone. But it wasn't her fault. They had done this to her. "Stop touching her!" I said.

"Why?" Colonel Selliwood said with a sinister smile. "I think she enjoys it."

I lunged forward but was quickly restrained ... by my own mother. She grabbed my arm and twisted it at a painful angle behind my back.

"Give up, Priscilla," Colonel Selliwood continued. "You won't win. As a matter of fact, I'm going to sit back and watch as your own mother kills you."

While I let those words settle on my brain, I felt my mother grab the back of my head and smash my face into a metal filing cabinet. I twisted out of her grasp nearly breaking my arm in the process. I ducked and missed a side kick she had aimed at my head, but then she quickly landed a windmill kick to the left side of my face. I thought I felt my jaw crack. When had my mother gotten so strong? Maybe she was always this strong and I had just never felt the full force of her abilities.

I stumbled across the room and landed with my side against the steel lab table that W was just on. The room was spinning as my mother came at me with cool yet scary and determined strides. She punched me in the stomach then sent an elbow to the side of my head. All I could do was hold up my hands to try to block the blows. I couldn't hit her back and run the risk of hurting baby Patricia. I fell to the floor as she kicked me repeatedly. There was something very dreamlike about being beaten to death by the woman who gave you life and was supposed to protect you. It didn't feel real. But the pain in my chest and stomach and just about everywhere else on my body, yes, that felt real.

"Samuel, don't you think this is a little cruel?" I heard Dr. Witherall say.

"Oh, shut up, Martin, I don't understand why you have such a soft spot for these two. If you had just killed them when I told you to, we wouldn't be in this situation. Specimen Delta, Specimen T, Specimen Gamma. That child over there has killed all three of them. She's a liability .... Oh, forget it. I'll shoot her myself." Colonel Selliwood held the gun up. "Specimen Q, fall back."

My mother stopped her assault on me, then calmly went to stand behind Colonel Selliwood like the perfect little soldier she was. Colonel Selliwood took a step toward me all the while holding a gun pointed at my head. This was it. There would be no bouncing bullets. Why hadn't I kissed Marco before I left?

Suddenly, Dr. Witherall came out of nowhere and knocked the gun away from Colonel Selliwood.

"What do you think you're doing, Martin?" Colonel Selliwood said.

"I'm tired of taking orders from you. This has gone too far. We're dealing with children here. Children! Specimen Q is pregnant. There is no telling the damage we've already done to the unborn fetus."

Colonel Selliwood stared at him with his eyes wide. Was he about to reach a turning point? Did the man have a heart after all?

"Specimen Q, kill Dr. Witherall," Colonel Selliwood said coldly.

I thought Witherall should have been scared or something as my mother turned toward him, but instead, he just smiled.

"Quinn, stand down," Dr. Witherall said. My mother obeyed and stared blankly in front of her. It was like she was a robot or something and only responded to commands.

"What's going on here?" Colonel Selliwood asked, a bead of sweat forming on his forehead.

"I rewrote the code to your programming. All the Specimens will respond to me over you."

"Martin, buddy," he said with a big cheesy grin and fake sincerity. "I know you're not going to do anything foolish. After all we've been through? We've been working on this for forty years. What's gotten into you?"

Dr. Witherall shrugged. "I don't know. Maybe I just want to be able to look in the mirror and not be disgusted with what I see. We've ruined so many lives."

Selliwood pulled out a small black object. It looked like a taser gun. My dad kept one like it in his nightstand. I tried to yell out a warning, but my voice came out a whisper. Selliwood aimed at Specimen W. Specimen W's body vibrated and the lights flickered on and off. We were left in complete darkness. Selliwood must have used the charge of the taser to activate Will Smith's powers and surge the electricity. He was getting away!

I tuned my hearing in the darkness and listened for his panicked footsteps. As he went for the door, I gathered all the reserve energy I had. I stood up and lunged for him. Unfortunately, in the darkness I tripped over W's body and fell flat on my face.

Colonel Selliwood got away.

In the darkness, Dr. Witherall found his way to a breaker box and got electricity back in the laboratory/office.

"Selliwood ... got ... away," I said, getting to my feet. I clutched my side and spit a mouthful of blood on the floor.

"I see that," Witherall said, grabbing some supplies out of cabinets. "We don't have much time. He's going to activate the transmitter."

I noticed my mother never moved throughout the whole ordeal. I don't think she even blinked. Dr. Witherall stood in front of her and said, "Quinn, power off."

My mother closed her eyes and slumped over.

"What are you doing to her?" I asked, aiming my hands at him. He may have just saved me, but if he was going to hurt my mother I would still toast his tail.

"Calm down, Priscilla. I'm helping you. I'm deactivating the chip."

I was a little shocked ... and confused ... and suspicious. Why had he decided to help me all of the sudden.

"But why?"

"For the same reason I told Colonel Selliwood. I don't want any more children hurt over my actions, especially ... my grandchildren."

"Whoa, wait, what? What do you mean grandchildren?"

Dr. Witherall sighed. "I'm Specimen Q's father. This makes you my granddaughter."

Chapter 24:
Open Head Surgery

I looked back and forth between my mother and Witherall looking for some sort of resemblance. Thankfully, there was none.

"Pick her up and put her on that table over there," he said. "Then check W's pulse and make sure he's alive."

I obeyed still reeling over this latest development. Did I hear him right? There had to be some kind of mistake. He must be confused.

After setting my mother on the table, Dr. Witherall set to work on her while I checked on W. His pulse was weak, but it was there. I went back over to my mother.

"Wait, let me make sure I understand this." I scratched my head in confusion. "You're my grandfather?"

Dr. Witherall nodded. "Yes, Priscilla. I volunteered my own genes to create your mother. It was just an experiment. I didn't expect it to even work. Specimen Q was the first successful fetus." Dr. Witherall shook his head. "I didn't know she was pregnant. If I'd known, I never would have —" He stopped abruptly.

"You never would have what?"

"The chip has been releasing a chemical in her brain ever since she left the Institute back in October. I'm sure she's been experiencing headaches and fatigue."

I nodded. So that was what was wrong with her all this time. I was glad I had an explanation but I just couldn't get this grandfather thing out of my head. And then a gross thought came in.

"Wait a minute. Did you only volunteer your ... whatever ... for my mother? Are you the father of any other Specimens ... namely Marco?" If he was Marco's dad too, that would mean I had made out with my ... uncle. Gross!

Dr. Witherall shook his head. "No, just your mother. She was the first. She was special."

I sighed in relief

He gently stroked my mother's red hair before saying, "I just hope the chemicals from the chip haven't affected the baby."

"Well, fix it. What do you need to do to fix it?" I suddenly wasn't thinking of my ... grandfather anymore. Instead I just wanted my baby sister to be okay.

He held up a black device to my mother's head. It looked like a simple DVD player remote.

"What was that?" I asked.

"I shut down the signal, but the chip still needs to be removed." He pulled a large needle out of a drawer then stuck it into my mother's head.

"Hey, what was that?"

"Local anesthetic. Don't worry. It won't hurt the baby. I need to make a small incision in her head in order to take out the chip. Pay attention to what I'm doing. You may need to do the same thing to the other kids."

"Me? You want me to cut people's heads open?"

"Yep." He kept working on my mother and explaining the delicate surgery. One slip of the knife could cause paralysis. I did a little nervous shiver. I didn't want to have that kind of responsibility. I hoped I would be able to explain the procedure to my dad and have him do it. "As soon as you find Peter and Katya, shut down the signal." He pointed toward the remote.

"Actually, Tai already interrupted the signal by modifying the Inhibitor Collars."

Dr. Witherall stared at me in surprise. "She did?"

I nodded.

"That's absolutely genius."

"I know right?"

"That should work for a while," he said going back to working on my mother, "but the transmitter from the magnetic North Pole may be able to override it. The chips still need to be removed."

"Great. So, I just gotta slice open my friends' heads. Got it. Can't wait."

"If Colonel Selliwood activates the transmitter, every Specimen with a chip in this building, in this country, in this world will be under his immediate control," Dr. Witherall said, ignoring my sarcasm. "It will be like he has a remote control that decides their immediate actions. You, Josh, and your friend Tai won't be affected, but you also won't be safe. Your friends will turn against you instantly and do whatever the colonel tells them to."

"Will I have to fight all of them?"

He nodded. "But you won't win. Not unless you disengage the transmitter."

"And how do I do that?"

Dr. Witherall stopped working on my mother and looked at me. "I created a kill switch in the system. Password Lenora. Remember that. Lenora. L-E-N-O-R-A." He spelled it out for me like I was some sort of idiot.

"I got it. What's a Lenora?"

"It's not a what, it's a who."

I thought back to the necklace he gave me for my birthday. I wondered if the L stood for this Lenora person. I wanted to know who she was, but I didn't think it was the right time.

"What's your escape plan?" Dr. Witherall asked, working on my mother's head again.

"Uh, yeah, I don't really have one."

"The entire base is tethered to the ocean floor kind of like a giant anchor," he explained. "The base was built above ground and made to float and then slowly brought under water. Break the tethers and it will float to the surface again."

"And just how do I break the tethers?"

"Go to Colonel Selliwood's computer," he said. "I'll show you."

Still clutching my side, I hobbled over to Selliwood's desk. Just then I heard something. It sounded like clicking heels and singing. And not just any kind of singing. Someone who had a strong British accent. Great. Not Xi.

"Xi's coming," I said, spinning around so fast I almost tripped and fell on my face ... again.

Dr. Witherall dropped the tiny metal microchip into a stainless steel dish then looked at me with panic. "I can't let her find you. That child is insane."

"You're telling me."

He quickly sewed up the cut and placed a bandage over it. Then he went to the other side of the room and activated the holographic wall. I could still see him, but he couldn't see me.

Xi entered the lab from the same door I did when I found Will Smith. She crossed her arms and glared at Dr. Witherall. Hey, she had her hands back. I wondered if I'd get a chance to slice them off again.

The scary looking Zero thing stood beside her and licked the back of his hand like he was a dog cleaning himself. In his other hand, he held a gun.

Wait a minute. Where was Marco? Did something happen to him? I felt like yelling through the holographic wall, but I couldn't risk it. I couldn't fight Xi and Zero while trying to protect my mother and Will Smith at the same time.

"Yeah, I'm gonna need you to get this thing out of my head," she said.

"What thing, Xi?" Dr. Witherall glanced nervously at the holographic wall. I wondered it Xi knew that the wall wasn't really there and that there was an office on the other side. If she knew, she didn't let on.

"The microchip. I want this microchip out of my head right now."

"I'm kind of busy —"

"Look, I know what you two are planning. I don't want to be some sort of robot. I need my own free will. I can't trust you people to pick out my outfits for me." Xi tossed her blond highlighted hair over her shoulder and smoothed a wrinkle in her red cashmere sweater. "Now, you're going to have to take this device out of my head immediately. I just saw Colonel Selliwood. He's planning on activating some magnet or signal or something so I assume that's what's going to take control of the microchip, right?"

"Xi, just come back later and I'll help you," Dr. Witherall said while trying to usher her out of the door. "I'm busy right now."

Xi looked around the room dramatically. "Hello, you don't look busy. Men." She rolled her eyes then buffed her fingernails on her shoulder. "I'll say it one more time using words you can understand," she spoke slowly as if speaking to a baby. "Take this thing out of my head or Zero here —" She looked at Zero for the first time. "What the devil are you doing? Are you licking yourself? God, I swear it's like having a dog for a partner." She snatched the gun away from him. "Just answer me," she continued as she pointed the gun at Dr. Witherall. "Are you going to remove the micro chip or not?"

Dr. Witherall shook his head slowly. "Maybe someone needs to control you, Xi. You are one sick little girl."

"Wrong answer." She nearly sang the words then pulled the trigger.

The bullet traveled as if in slow motion into his head. He collapsed to the ground. I had to cover my mouth to hold in a gasp. She'd killed him. She had shot him dead right before my eyes. A few hours ago, I might not have minded that. I might have even been happy. But Dr. Witherall was my grandfather. And he had just saved my life ... and my mother's life ... and hopefully my baby sister's life. My heart squeezed tighter and tighter in my chest. I thought I would explode. I had to fight to hold in my emotions.

"If you want something done right," she said grabbing a scalpel from the shelf, "you have to do it yourself." Next Xi did something even more shocking than shooting someone dead at point blank range. I knew she was crazy. I knew she was completely insane, but I didn't know how deep the insanity went.

Xi jammed the scalpel into her head. I shielded my eyes when I saw the blood splatter. She might not be able to feel pain, but the sight of her digging into her scalp was painful for me just to watch. I thought I was going to pass out.

After a few seconds, I peeked through my fingers to see what she was doing. She had sliced open the side of her head and was using a mirror to get a close up look at ... at ... Was that her brain? Ugh. I felt nauseated, but I couldn't turn away.

Xi soon figured out that she was working on the wrong side of her head. As soon as she removed the scalpel, the open wound started healing itself. She then sliced open the other side.

Finally, she found what she was looking for. The tiny microchip transmitter had a light that blinked. When she dug her fingers into her head to yank it out something unexpected happened. Her legs gave way and she passed out.

Specimen Zero took a step forward and nudged her with his foot. When she didn't move, he knelt down and sniffed her. Wait a minute. Did he actually sniff her? Anyway, Zero started yelping. I didn't understand why he was so attached to Xi.

With Xi incapacitated and Zero occupied mourning her, it was the perfect time to escape. But I knew I wouldn't get far carrying my mom and Will Smith. And what if another specimen came around? I needed reinforcements.

Chapter 25:
Tai the Terrific

Josh, are you there? I called him in my mind. He didn't respond. I really sucked at telepathy. I was totally telepathetic. I would have to remember to get some lessons from my mother if we ever got out of this. Maybe she could teach me to be telepathic.

I ran shaky fingers through my hair. I had just seen my grandfather shot at point blank range by a psychopath who then sliced open her own head! I had two incapacitated genetically-enhanced assassins who I cared about waiting for me to save them. My stomach started turning. What was I gonna do? How was I gonna get out of here? My grand ... Dr. Witherall didn't even have a chance to show me how to get the base to float to the surface. What if we all died in this underwater coffin?

I fell to the floor and put my head in my hands. I had to force myself to calm down. Freaking out wasn't going to help anyone.

I needed Josh. Whenever I was about to have a Prissy Fit, he was able to send me this calm feeling that instantly made me feel better.

Josh? Josh, where are you? If you're dead, I'll kill you. Once again completely illogical, but whatever.

I glanced at my watch. I was supposed to meet Marco at the loading dock in two minutes. I needed to get moving. I knew I was strong enough to carry both of them, I just hoped I didn't run into any specimens along the way.

I had just tossed Will Smith over my shoulder when I heard someone trying to burst through the door. I looked through the holographic wall at Specimen Zero. He'd heard it too. He yelped then ran away. Once again. What a wimp!

The banging continued. I didn't know who it was, but they were about to face a fight. I placed Will back on the ground and braced myself for an attack. After one more loud bang, a streak of silver burst through the door.

"Marco?" I didn't wait for a response. I just ran into his arms.

"I'm so glad you're okay," he said, hugging me back.

"Where's Josh?"

He started to say something and then stopped. He looked around the room. "What happened to them?" he asked, pointing to Dr. Witherall and Xi through the holographic wall.

"Witherall is dead. Xi killed him. Then she stabbed herself in the head trying to get her microchip out herself. She's been out cold for like five minutes. But she can come to any second. We should probably try to get out of here. Wait a minute," I said. "You didn't answer my question. Where's Josh? Did something happen to him?"

Marco wouldn't make eye contact with me as he said. "He's going to be fine."

"Going to be fine? What happened?" I started to panic. I had come here to save my mother. I didn't want to lose my brother in the process.

"Calm down. He really will be fine."

"Just tell me."

He sighed. "We can walk and talk," he said gently lifting my mother from the table as if she was small sleeping child. Then he turned and headed toward the door.

I picked up Will again, tossed him over my shoulder and followed.

"I was chasing after Zero hoping he'd lead me to Selliwood when I got a telepathic distress call from Josh," Marco explained as we made our way through the narrow hallways. "I gave up on Zero and went to find Josh. He and Tai were locked in a room surrounded by guards. He was controlling eight guards and Specimen Beta with his powers when I showed up to help. Beta alone would be enough to exhaust him. He passed out from the strain, but he should be fine soon."

I breathed a sigh of relief. I knew how much it took out of him to use his hypnotic suggestion on just regular humans. I couldn't imagine how much it took to control another specimen.

"You should probably be more concerned about your friend, Taiana. She was, how do you say, 'totally freaked out?'"

I could only imagine. This was so far beyond anything she had ever done before. I wonder if she regretted coming with me now.

We turned a corner and went through a door into a room filled with tied up guards. That must have been how Marco subdued them. Even after being trained as an assassin for most of his life, he refused to use deadly force. All the guys were alive and well, but probably a little embarrassed for getting beat by an unarmed teenager.

Josh and Tai were in a glass compartment in the middle of the room. It kind of looked like they were in a fish tank or something.

"Josh!" I cried when I saw him lying unconscious on the floor. Tai held his head in her lap as she cried uncontrollably. I lay Will down then knelt beside Josh and felt for his pulse. Marco put my mother down next to both of them.

"It's all my fault," Tai continued. "I should have worked faster. We could've been out of here before the guards showed up and Josh wouldn't have had to use his powers. He was just trying to protect me."

"He's got a pulse," I said. "Josh! Josh, can you hear me?" I yelled before giving him a hard slap across the face.

Josh groaned then started humming *Genie in a Bottle* by Christina Aguilera. Yeah, he was going to be fine.

Suddenly, a loud noise erupted all around us. I covered my ears and fell to the floor. The piercing buzz was so loud I thought sure it would shatter the glass of the room we were in. It was beyond piercing. It was like a buzzing sound wrapped up in a screech and topped off with a ringing.

"Priss, what's wrong?" Tai asked.

What kind of a question was that? Didn't she hear it? I looked up at her. She seemed completely unaffected by the painfully loud noise. I guess she didn't hear it. I looked over at Marco. He seemed confused as to why I was covering my ears.

"Don't you hear that?" I asked, looking between both of them.

Marco shook his head. "It must be your super hearing."

I screamed in pain then curled up into the fetal position.

"Priscilla, how can I help you?" Marco asked, kneeling beside me.

"Make it stop! Just make it stop!" I was near tears it hurt so badly.

"But I don't know what it is?" Marco sounded helpless.

"Signal. It's the signal," Josh whispered. His eyes were still closed. I couldn't quite figure out if he was waking up or sleep talking.

I tried to register what Josh was saying. Had Colonel Selliwood enacted the transmitter? Was it projecting on a frequency only I could hear with my super hearing? If that was the case it would mean —

A hard punch to my face interrupted my thoughts. Then suddenly I was flying through the air. I crashed through a glass window of the compartment and landed against the wall on the other side of the room. I looked up to see Marco standing over me with a vicious look in his eye. He had punched me and thrown me across the room. I looked in his eyes again. This wasn't Marco. This wasn't the boy who only minutes ago said he would do anything for me. This person inside Marco's metal body would do only one thing: Kill me.

Chapter 26:
Chips activated

I rubbed the side of my face with one hand while using my other arm to block a kick to my face. I grabbed his metal leg and threw him against the wall. He seemed totally unfazed as he reached out with two quick punches to my face and stomach.

I was dizzy and unstable. I felt blood pooling in my mouth. The ridiculously loud noise continued, making it feel like sharp objects were being crammed in my ears. I needed a second to get myself together. I threw a desk at Marco's head as I ran and hid behind some sort of electronic control board a few feet away from where Josh and Tai were.

"How did Selliwood turn on the transmitter? Wouldn't he have to do it from this room?" I asked Tai from my hiding place. I knew I only had a few seconds before Marco came at me again. Probably less time than that. I just needed to wrap my head around what was going on.

"He must have some sort of remote," she said in a loud whisper. I should have told her whispering wouldn't matter. Marco could read our minds if he wanted to. I stole a quick glance at him, walking around in circles looking for me. Strange. Turning on the microchip must have subdued some of his other natural abilities. He was like a mindless robot, without the ability to think for himself and use logic to find me. Maybe he didn't have use of his telepathy anymore.

"Can you turn it off?" I asked.

"I don't know," she said, hugging my brother's limp body closer.

I didn't hear Marco's metal footsteps coming toward me. Instead, they were getting further away. I poked my head around and saw him headed toward Tai and Josh with a slow and determined stride.

"Oh no you don't!" I yelled, leaping up and shooting a stream of fire toward him.

He screamed in pain as his metal body started turning red from the flame.

I felt bad for hurting him, but what else was I supposed to do? I couldn't let him get to Tai and Josh.

After a few seconds of my fire power, Marco ran away, quickly disappearing with his super speed. An instant later, Marco's left fist connected with my right eye. I hadn't even seen him coming!

I did a backflip out of the way trying to buy some time before I would actually have to fight him back. I stole a glance at Tai, who had made her way to the computer to try to figure out how to undo whatever had been done to Marco.

"How's it going over there, Tai?"

"I'm doing the best I can."

"I don't know how long I can hold him off, Tai. He's —" I didn't get to finish my thought as Marco landed a right hook to the side of my face. My mouth filled with the metallic taste of blood. Deciding I was sick of getting beat up, I reared back and landed a punch to his gut. "OW!" I cried out in pain. I almost broke my hand!

I threw a blast of fire at him with my good hand to give myself a chance to get away. I hid behind a table and tried to think. What was I going to do? I couldn't fight him. Not unless I wanted to break every bone in my body. My only chance was fire. And I had to do it fast. I had to keep him away from Tai so she'd have time to work and figure things out. I focused my hearing and heard his metal footsteps just to my left.

Leaping out from my hiding place, I started blasting him with my fire power. His screams of pain almost made me stop immediately. I really didn't want to hurt him but I had no choice. He fell to one knee, still crying out in agony. I thought I had done enough so I stopped shooting. A second later, however, he disappeared. Now it was my turn to spin around in confused circles. Where did he go? Well, that stupid question was painfully answered as soon as I felt his metal fingers around my neck.

I gasped as I tried to scratch, hit, and kick my way free. Nothing worked. He was squeezing the life out of me. I started blasting his face with fire, but I had so little oxygen in my lungs I didn't have the energy. The stream was weak and started to fade.

The only thing that kept me going was thinking of Kyle and how much I wanted to see him again one day. That was what gave me the burst of energy to shoot streams of fire into both of Marco's ears. He released my neck and clutched the sides of his head.

I ran away and hid again while gasping for air and rubbing my sore neck.

"Uh, Priss. We've got company," Tai said as I turned around and around trying to find where Marco had gone.

"What do you mean?"

"According to this monitor, Ian is coming this way. And I don't think he likes us very much anymore."

"What's your point? He never liked us!" I yelled as I frantically searched for Marco.

"Uh, my point is he looks about as deadly as Marco right now. And he's leading the others right to us!"

Tai must have meant Katya, Ian, Peter, and Ryan. Their chips were probably activated as well.

Just then, I noticed a streak of silver running in circles around the room. He must have been trying to cool himself off before attacking me again.

And then there was the added problem of Katya, Ian, Peter, and Ryan. There was no way I could fight them alone. I actually contemplated letting some of the tied up guards go so they could help me. But who's to say they wouldn't just run away leaving me all alone again. How was I gonna get out of this?

"Tai, you gotta figure out how to turn that thing off. It's our only chance."

"Don't you think I'm working on that?"

The silver streak passed me again. I shot out a flame, but missed him.

"I'm in the system. I'm just not sure I know how to shut it down," Tai said.

I shot another flame and heard a screech of pain. Got him.

"Wait a minute," I said as a thought popped into my head. "Witherall! He put in a kill switch. Type in the word 'Lenora.'" In my excitement over remembering the kill switch thing, I turned around and looked at Tai. Big mistake. I felt a kick to the back of my head that sent me face first into more glass.

"It's not working," Tai said frantically. "There's some sort of biometric key."

"What does that mean?" I asked, rolling over, narrowly missing Marco's next attack. I jumped up to start running again when I tripped over a chair and fell to the floor. Marco was barreling down on me getting ready for a kill when, suddenly, he fell backwards. How did that happen? I looked over and saw that Josh had come to long enough to literally pull the rug out from underneath Marco.

"It means only someone with Dr. Witherall's DNA can start the sequence," Josh breathed.

I jumped up and burned Marco again with all the strength I could muster. Once Marco was securely melted to the floor, I jumped over him and went to where Tai was working frantically at the computer terminal.

"What do I do? What do I press?" I asked.

"What do you mean? Didn't you hear Josh? Only someone with Dr. Witherall's DNA can —"

"I'll explain later," I said, cutting her off. "Just tell me what to press."

"Put your left hand here and keep it there while you type Lenora."

"Door," Josh said, his voice still a whisper.

I looked over at the main door just in time to see Ian walk through it. Not wanting to see his nakedness, I turned around and reached for Josh's gun.

"Here," I said, stuffing it into Tai's chest. "Aim for the door and don't stop shooting till I tell you."

Tai took the gun in her shaky hands and aimed for the door. Tears streaking down her face, she fired at Ian who was unlocking the door to let the others in.

I placed my left hand on the scanner looking thing. I felt a prick at the bottom of my thumb. Then a box appeared on the computer screen. I assumed that was where I needed to type the password. So I did.

L-E-N-O-R-A

The loud buzzing stopped. The pain slowly eased out of my brain. Naked, Ian grabbed his head and fell to the floor. He blinked rapidly as if someone had just shone a bright light in his face.

It worked. It was over. Except, I still heard bullets bouncing off of the ceiling. I looked over and saw Tai still shooting. Wow, that girl had horrible aim. I think I needed to put her through some sort of sidekick boot camp.

"You can stop shooting now, Tai. It's over." I pried the gun out of her hands. She dropped to her knees crying. I wrapped an arm around her and hugged her. "Good work, Tai. Good work."

227

Chapter 27:
This Sinks

We scooped Marco off of the floor with a make shift spatula and a few strategically placed flames from my fingers. It probably hurt like heck. Pieces of his metal body stayed firmly attached to the floor. He was sure to have open sores when he reverted back to human form.

"I'm so sorry, Priscilla," he said through clenched teeth as he sat on a lab table. "I saw myself hitting you and I couldn't stop. I never meant to hurt you." He gently touched my bruised face.

"Ditto," I said, rubbing the now misshapen metal on his arms.

"Don't worry; I'll revert back to my normal form in a few moments."

"Aren't you going to be bruised?"

He nodded. "Badly."

"I'm sorry."

He put a slightly melted finger to my lips. "You did what you had to do."

"I hate to interrupt this little love fest," a now fully clothed Ian said as he massaged his temples, "but we still need to figure out a way to get out of here."

"We are 300 feet below the surface. Colonel Selliwood and three of the Specimens took the last escape pod," Katya said, kneeling next to my brother. Tai crossed her arms and glared at Katya stroking Josh's hair.

"I missed you so much," Josh said as he pulled her into a hug. A few seconds later, he passed out again.

I noticed both Katya and Peter were still a little hazy. Peter was leaning against his twin for support and Katya kept shaking her head every couple of seconds as if to clear her thoughts. I bet their heads were still swimming from having their chips activated, then neutralized by the collar then over powered again by the transmitter.

Hmm. Swimming. I glanced through a portal window into the Arctic water. Would we have to swim our way out of here? I looked around the room. Will, Josh, and my mom were completely incapacitated and wouldn't be able to swim. Peter and Katya weren't that much better. Even though Ryan and Ian were in pretty good shape right now, they'd probably still freeze to death. And Marco, well if Marco went into the water in his metal state, he'd just sink.

Will Smith was slowly coming around. He was tossing and turning in the spot where I laid him a few minutes ago. I wondered how long it would be until he could help with this mission. My mother was still out cold. It would probably take her a few hours to recover from the surgery Dr. Witherall had performed.

"Dr. Witherall told me that the base was attached to the ocean floor by two tethers," I said to Tai, the only other person not passed out or recovering from brainwashing. "He said if the tethers were broken, the base would float to the top. He didn't have a chance to tell me how to break them though."

Tai looked at me with one eyebrow raised. "So Dr. Witherall gave you the code to deactivate the transmitter and he told you how to escape? Why was he being so nice to you? And why did the biometric scanner accept your DNA?"

I took a deep breath and said, "Because Dr. Witherall is my grandfather."

Ryan, Peter, Ian, Katya, Tai, and Marco just stared at me with eyes wide.

"No way. That can't be true," Ryan said.

"It's true. He donated his genes to create my mother."

"Are we related to him as well?" Peter asked. I didn't realize how much I missed his little Norwegian accent until he spoke for the first time.

"No, just my mother. The rest of the specimens had different parents."

Marco let out an audible sigh of relief. He was probably thinking the same thing I was about him possibly being my uncle. Gross.

"That explains why your DNA worked. But who or what is Lenora?" Tai asked.

I shrugged. "No clue."

***

Tai brought up a picture of the base from below on the computer. I got a good look at the tethers locking the base in place. She couldn't find any mechanism for releasing them.

I sighed and pushed away from the computer. "Well, since we can't figure out how to break the tethers from inside, I guess I'm going in." I started opening cabinets looking for an oxygen tank.

"What?" Marco said, leaping from the table and grabbing my arm. "You can't do that, you'll freeze to death."

"Of all of us, I'm probably the only one guaranteed not to freeze. I'm a human fireball, remember?" I lit a flame with my right hand for emphasis.

He opened his mouth to say something, but quickly closed it again when he realized he couldn't dispute that. "Well, I'm coming with you," he said finally.

"That's pointless Marco. You're an extremely dense metal right now. If you were to go into the water, you'd just sink to the bottom."

He closed his eyes and took a deep breath. He knew I was right. He knew I had to do this alone.

I found an oxygen tank packed away in a closet to the left of the main entrance of the room. I didn't want to take any chances of running out of air and not being able to complete this mission. I memorized the location and consistency of the tethers from the images Tai brought up on the computer. They were made of layers of wires surrounded by a metal casing. They shouldn't be too hard for me to break. I just needed to make sure I broke both of them within a short amount of time. If I broke one and not the other, one side of the base would start rising while the other would be held down.

As I jumped in, the freezing water hit me like millions of tiny little knives. With a little concentration, I

233

made my body pulse with heat and regulated my body temperature.

A huge fat walrus swam past me. It was pretty ugly yet kind of beautiful at the same time. If I didn't have a life or death mission to complete, I might have taken the time to admire the beautiful plant and animal life underwater. But as it was, I swam with determination through the dark water, past sea creatures big and small toward my target.

I reached the metal chain that hooked into the bottom of the base after only about fifteen seconds. I gave it a good hard yank but couldn't pull it free. It was stronger than I thought. I focused my energy and tugged at it again. This time it came free. The left side of the base started slowly floating up. The other tether was about two football field lengths away. I needed to swim over there and loosen that chain before the entire base became vertical.

I started my swim when I noticed the walrus again. I tried to swim past it, but it got right in front of me. When I tried to go around it, it pushed me. Did I just get pushed by a walrus? Why was a walrus trying to pick a fight with me?

I pushed it back and tried to swim above it when it jabbed me in the stomach with its huge blubbery tail. Then it stabbed me in the shoulder with its tusk. The pain was almost as insane as the idea of a walrus kicking my butt. I took a look in its eyes. I recognized that stupid vacant stare. This was no walrus. It was Specimen Zero.

He must have borrowed some DNA from the walrus I had seen earlier. I wondered if Xi had come to and put him up to this. Xi would have jumped in herself in order to fight me, but she probably didn't want to ruin her hair.

My tank had plenty of air, so I wasn't worried about losing oxygen and dying. And I was pretty sure that once I was able to focus, I could defeat a walrus, but in watching one side of the base float up I was afraid that soon everyone inside would be sliding over to one side. I needed to act quickly.

I don't know how much time passed as I exchanged jabs with this massive sea creature, but slowly, I was starting to panic. The base was nearly straight up and down. I had to think of something to get away from this animal once and for all.

Just then, I saw Marco awkwardly dive into the water near the other tether. He started dropping ... rapidly. On his way down, he grabbed onto the chain. His weight actually made the base start sinking again. He gave it a tug and pulled it free. The base instantly started floating upward. Marco on the other hand was sinking and fast. He was too heavy to swim. What was he thinking?

I had to get away from Zero and save Marco. I took a deep breath and then snatched off my oxygen tank. I jammed it into Zero's mouth. I released the valve and sent the Zero walrus sailing away.

I turned and saw Marco still sinking. I tried to send him a telepathic message. It didn't work. Why didn't I have telepathy? *Read my mind, Marco. Read my mind and know that I'm coming for you.*

I dove toward him. "Marco!" I tried to scream. I don't know what I was thinking. Who screams in the water? I had stupidly managed to squeeze out the last bit of oxygen in my lungs. Well, I kind of do know what I was thinking. Marco was sinking and there was no way for me to get to him especially without an oxygen tank. But I was going to try. There was no way I would let him die. I dove toward him. The water was dark, but I could still see a solid metal shape in the distance.

My starving lungs were begging for air. I didn't know how long I had been without my oxygen tank. It was getting harder and harder to swim. I felt weak. My arms and legs were moving as hard and fast as I could push them but it felt like I wasn't going anywhere. I couldn't see Marco's silver form anymore. All I saw was darkness.

I finally gave in to my lung's desire and tried to breathe. My chest burned as it filled with ice cold water. Everything went black.

Chapter 28:
Alive

"Marco!" I yelled, gasping for air. Where was the water? Why wasn't I cold? I looked around. I wasn't in the Arctic Ocean any more.

"We're in a United States Military hospital on a base in Norway," my mother said, leaping from a recliner and coming to stand next to me.

"Where's Marco?" My throat was dry. My tongue felt like leather. I tried to sit up, but my mother laid me back down.

"Just relax, sweetie. You've been unconscious for a long time."

"How long?"

"Three days."

She answered that question easy enough, why wouldn't she answer my other one? Maybe I didn't really want to know the answer.

"Where's Marco?" I asked again louder and more forcefully.

My mother took a deep breath. "I'm so sorry, sweetie."

I turned over in the bed. I didn't want to be alive without Marco. Why didn't I die too?

***

For three days, all I saw in my head was Marco's metal shape floating away from me. And there was nothing I could do. Why wasn't I strong enough to save him? Why couldn't I break the tethers on my own so that he didn't have to come out and help me? It was all my fault. Marco was dead and it was all my fault.

"It's not your fault," my mother said as if she read my mind. She probably did read my mind. I had to keep remembering that she had her powers back. It was going to take some getting used to.

She sat on the edge of my hospital bed and grabbed my hand. I tensed a little. The last time my mother had touched me, she was trying to kill me. I had to remind myself that she was back to normal ... well, normal for her.

"It's not your fault, Prissy. You did everything you could. You did your best." She stroked my hair softly.

I turned over and looked at her. "That doesn't make me feel better, Mom. It just lets me know that my best isn't good enough."

My mother had tears in her eyes. "What have I done to you? I've put too much pressure on you. This isn't your fight. You never should have been involved."

She stood up and walked over to the window.

"I'm just glad it's over now," she said, hugging herself. "We can go back to being a family."

"Where are Dad and the boys and Katya and Tai?" I asked, sitting up in the hospital bed.

"The boys are in Missouri," she said. "Josh was still pretty incapacitated after using his powers. The doctors never would've been able to figure out what was wrong with him. He's been resting at home since. Tai is back in River's Bend. Katya went to New Zealand for a while to visit with Ian."

I groaned at the sound of his name. I was just happy he was half a world away.

"I understand you and Ian didn't get along too well," she said with a smirk.

I nodded, not wanting to waste my breath explaining what a jerk he'd been since the second I saw his naked butt hiding behind a frying pan.

"Well, he saved your life."

"Whoa. Wait. What?"

"You heard me. If it wasn't for him, you wouldn't be alive. He fished you out of the ocean and then revived you with CPR."

I know I should have been immediately grateful, but my first thought was, ew gross. His lips were actually on mine.

"Um, wow. I guess I should probably thank him or something."

My mother took a deep breath and closed her eyes. For a moment, I just focused on her eyeballs dancing around under her lids. What in the world was she doing?

"He says you're welcome," she said after opening her eyes and exhaling.

I smiled a little inside. My mother had her powers back. At least one thing was back to normal. Well, if you consider someone being able to talk to someone in New Zealand in their mind normal.

I looked down at the needle sticking out of my hand and followed the tube up to a bag hanging over my head." What's that?" I asked.

"Mostly nutrients. You haven't eaten or drunken anything in three days. There are also a few chemicals to neutralize your powers."

I sat up again. "So the doctors here know? Won't they ask too many questions? I thought we had to keep everything a secret. You shouldn't have brought me to a hospital."

She turned and smiled at me. "It's good to have friends in high places, I guess."

"What are you talking about?"

"Elizabeth Gonzalez, the president's daughter. Katya brought back her memories of how you saved her. Her father pulled some strings for us. Let's just say, we're here, but we're not really here, if you know what I mean."

My head hurt too much to try to figure out what she was getting at. I just assumed that somehow after I left this hospital no one would ever figure out that I was ever here or that I was any different from any other thirteen-year-old.

"Elizabeth was also able to help us make sure that Colonel Selliwood went away for a long time. He'll never bother us again."

"Wait. They caught him?"

My mother nodded. "When Specimen W came to, he and Tai were able to hack into his private computer system and reveal all the evidence against Selliwood for his past offenses, including kidnapping Elizabeth. They even tracked his escape pod and the National Guard caught him off the New England coast. Selliwood faces a sentence of life in prison in a maximum security facility. It's over, sweetie."

Over? It was really over? I had to admit, I was a little upset that I wasn't the one to capture him. I really wanted just one chance to wrap my fingers around his neck and make him beg for mercy. Did that make me evil? I wasn't sure. I just knew that somehow, I still didn't feel complete. Something was missing. Or I guess that something could've been Marco.

I couldn't cry. It was like crying would make me have to accept Marco's death. If I didn't cry and I wasn't sad, then maybe I could convince myself that it wasn't true. If I just kept telling myself that Marco wasn't dead and that he was at the safe house trying to find a puzzle piece that I had hidden from him then maybe it would come true.

"I think we should talk," my mother said on the flight back to Missouri.

"About what?" I said, crossing my arms. I hadn't said much since I'd woken up from my little coma. I didn't have much to say. I certainly didn't want to talk about what happened at Crang. It just reminded me of Marco. Everything reminded me of him.

"I'm sorry about what I did ... to you and to your father," she said, looking straight ahead into the night.

"I know." And I did know. I knew my mother loved me. I knew she loved my father. And I knew that under normal circumstances, she would not have tried to kill either one of us.

"I just feel so awful about what I did to you and what happened to —"

"Mom!" I said, interrupting her before she brought up Marco. "I don't want to talk about this right now." I didn't think I'd ever be able to talk about it.

Chapter 29:
The Worst Superhero Ever

I came home to a hero's welcome. There was a banner hanging in the living room, confetti flying in my face, flowers everywhere, and my dad had even baked a cake.

"You guys didn't have to do all this," I said when I walked in. Although it did make me feel really good inside that they went through all this trouble. I felt a little like a celebrity in my own home.

"Of course we did," my dad said sweeping me into a giant bear hug. "We're so proud of you, Prissy."

"Welcome back, Prissy!" Charlie and Chester yelled while attacking my legs with hugs.

My father set me down then looked at my mother. "Quinn," he said with a nod.

"Greg," she replied.

I looked back and forth between them. What was up with the cold greeting? Usually they were all over each other, especially if my mother was away for a few days because of a mission.

"We have another surprise for you," my dad said turning his attention back to me.

"Really, what?" Even though I was still depressed about Marco, I was started to get a little excited. I mean who doesn't get happy inside at the mention of a surprise?

My dad stood behind me and covered my eyes. Even on the carpet, I could hear feet moving. Someone was coming into the living room. When my dad moved his hands, Elizabeth Gonzalez stood in front of me.

"Elizabeth!" I yelled.

"Priss!" she screamed as we hugged each other.

"It's so good to see you," I said. That was totally true. A few months ago, when I saved her from

Selliwood, we only got to hang out for a couple of hours. But in that short time, we totally clicked. I knew she was a cool chick.

"Big ditto, girl. I'm so happy I was able to help your family after you, you know, saved my life and all."

***

"So how are you really doing?" Elizabeth said as we hung out by the swing set in our backyard.

"What do you mean? I'm fine." I sat down in one of the swings and gently rocked back and forth.

Out of the corner of my eye, I could see Elizabeth shake her head as she sat next to me.

"Marco's dead," she said matter-of-factly. "I saw the way you looked at him the day you saved my life. I know you're not fine."

I didn't respond.

We sat in silence for a while as we rocked back and forth and stared at the sunset.

"When I was ten, my uncle died while fighting in Iraq."

I stopped rocking in the swing and stared at her.

"I was devastated," she continued. "I remembered the first Christmas without him. I waited by the window still expecting him to walk up our driveway with a bag of my favorite chocolate candy."

"How did you get over it?" I asked.

She shrugged. "I didn't. You never do. Every day, you wake and you figure out a way to make it through. Some days it's easy. Other days you're in the candy aisle of the grocery story bawling over a bag of Rollo's."

I took a deep breath and let it out slowly. I really appreciated how she was trying to make me feel better, but I couldn't help but feel like she didn't really understand. I mean, she wasn't in Iraq when her uncle died. She didn't have the power to save him and yet fail miserably. Her uncle's death wasn't her fault. Marco's death was totally my fault. I was the worst superhero ever.

"I know what you're thinking and it's not your fault."

I snapped my head up and looked at her. "How did you know what I was thinking?" I searched my brain for a second to make sure she wasn't in there. For a moment, I thought she had some psychic powers or something.

She smiled a little. "No, I didn't read your mind. It's just written all over your face. You blame yourself for Marco's death and you shouldn't. You've saved so many people. Me included. You're amazing, Priss. Don't ever forget that."

She stood up and wrapped her arm around me. One of her Secret Service agents took a protective step forward.

"Would you chill?" she called out to him. "I'm just trying to hug her."

I hugged her back and said, "You're pretty amazing yourself." She really had succeeded at making me feel better. I couldn't believe that the actual daughter of the President had traveled all the way to Middle-of-Nowhere, Missouri just to make me feel better. There had to be a way to show her how much I appreciated her help. Then I remembered the last time we were together. She desperately wanted to be a part of "Super kid club" or whatever and to not have her memory erased. There really wasn't a club or anything, but for all she'd done, I figured I could create one for her. So I said. "It was pretty amazing how you were able to get us set up in that military hospital, no questions asked. You could be totally useful for us. How about we make you an honorary Super Kid?"

She pulled away. "Really? Shut up! Really? No way."

"Yes way."

"Can I have a secret code name too, like La Escondida or La Comandita.?"

"Yeah, sure, whatever you want," I said, trying to keep myself from giggling at her excitement.

"This is so cool. Do you guys have a secret handshake or something?"

"Um, yeah sure," I said, taking her hand and making up a spontaneous series of hand movements. It ended up looking like a cross between throwing gang signs and a sign language version of a bird call. It wasn't that bad though. I'd have to remember to teach it to Tai.

Chapter 30:
The Truth About Josh

I was so busy having fun with Elizabeth and making up secrets code names and phrases that I almost didn't notice how Josh hadn't said a word to me all day. I just came out of a three day coma and my own brother hadn't even said 'welcome home' or 'good to see you' or anything. It was strange.

Was he avoiding me? I mean every time I entered a room, he'd find an excuse to leave. I thought maybe he was embarrassed that he couldn't help me at Crang. Maybe he felt he should've been the one to get me out of the ocean and revive me. I thought that had to be the reason. But then the next day when Katya came back from New Zealand I figured it all out.

Josh and Katya hugged for like ten minutes straight. He buried his head in her hair and took deep breaths as if he was addicted to nicotine and she was a fresh cigarette.

That's when it hit me. I knew exactly why he was avoiding me. It all made perfect sense now.

I waited until that night before I confronted him. The twins were asleep. Peter, Ryan and Katya were in the safe house. Mom and Dad were in their bedroom arguing. I'll talk about that later.

From the kitchen doorway, I crossed my arms and stared at my older brother. We didn't always agree on things, but we had always been able to understand each other. Whenever we fought we always quickly forgave each other. I didn't know if I could ever forgive him for this.

Josh had gotten into the habit of watching a blank television screen for hours on end. He said it helped clear his head and lead to more visions. I wondered if this was the same place where he got the vision that was about to drive a wedge between us.

"You knew didn't you?" I asked Josh after staring at him for like ten minutes.

"I knew what?" he asked, picking up the remote. I could tell he was nervous the way he pointed the wrong end of it toward the TV.

"Marco. You knew he was going to die on that mission, didn't you?"

Josh gave up on the remote and set it down on the coffee table. He clasped his hands together and stared at his fingers. "Yeah, I knew."

"God, Josh! Why didn't you tell me?" I stomped into the living room and kicked the coffee table breaking it in half. Josh closed his eyes and turned his head.

"I wasn't sure, okay? My visions have been off lately."

"But you could have warned me. Why didn't you say something? Anything. How could you do this to me?"

"What would you have done differently, Priss? Can you honestly say that it would have changed anything?"

"Yes! No! I don't know. But I would have done something differently. There's no way I would have —"

"What? Would you have not gone? Would you have left Mom and Peter and Katya under Selliwood's control?" Josh stood up and towered over me. It was hard to believe that he was so much bigger than me but I would still be able to knock him out cold in a matter of seconds if need be.

"Katya, huh," I said, crossing my arms and staring up at him. "That's what this is really about, isn't?"

"What are you talking about?"

"You know exactly what I'm talking about." I continued to glare at him. The fire in my eyes burned through him to the truth. Finally, he couldn't take it anymore and he turned away. I was right. He didn't tell me because he was afraid I wouldn't have gone and saved Katya. "Do you know what you've done, Josh? You sacrificed my boyfriend for your girlfriend."

"You know that's not true. Marco was my friend, too. I'm hurting too, you know?"

"You've been manipulating me the whole time. Making me think this was my mission and that I was in charge. You knew what was going to happen the whole time. You probably just wanted me to blame myself for what happened to Marco!"

"Come on, Priss. Calm down. That's not true!"

Josh reached out to hug me but I slapped his hands away.

"You are not my brother. I hate you, Josh," I said before storming off to my room.

Chapter 31:
Another Break Up

My father never liked hospitals. He didn't like all the questions they had to ask. What's your name? Where do you live? How did you get that stab wound in your chest? So when Dad rushed Mom to the hospital in the middle of the night a few weeks after Crang, I knew it had to be serious. I new baby Patricia had to be in trouble.

When I found out she died, I put her memorial right next to where I built one for Marco. I visited it every day and left a flower or a poem for them. It was my secret way of dealing with my grief. I thought about making one for Dr. Witherall as well. I mean, technically, he was my grandfather and he had saved me from Colonel Selliwood. But I still couldn't get over all the other things he had done. Not yet anyway. My mother had no idea he was her biological father all this time, though now it made sense why he had refused to kill her on so many occasions. He just couldn't bring himself to harm his own child.

Everyone probably thought I was the strong super hero I was supposed to be as I hid away all my emotions. Josh and I weren't speaking. The twins were too young to talk to about serious stuff like this. And my parents were going through too many problems of their own to worry about me. I felt so alone.

I hoped my parents would try again and make another baby. I was so used to the idea of having a sister that I couldn't get over the fact that she was gone.

I was being selfish. True, I had lost a sister and it really hurt, but my parents had lost a child. Unfortunately, I also think they lost a piece of each other. They would go days without talking and then when they were forced to say something to each other, it always turned into a fight.

One night, I overheard one of their arguments.

"I can't live like this anymore, Quinn," my dad said.

"Like what? We can be a family again. The worst is over. Selliwood is in jail — "

"Until he escapes or something and comes after us again. What about all the specimens still out there that are on his side, huh? Specimen Xi, Specimen Zero, Specimen Theta, Specimen Z to name a few. How long before one of them breaks him out of jail and we're back to where we started? I don't want to put my family in danger anymore."

There was a pause.

"What are you saying, Greg?"

My dad didn't respond.

"I love you so much, Greg."

"I love you, too. I just ... I can't ... I can't take this. My baby ... our baby is gone." Then they both started crying.

Around this time of stress for my parents, I turned into a class A stalker. Were stalkers divided into classes? Whatever. Anyway, I became obsessed with following Kyle's career. As the face of Mini Frosted Funnel Cakes, he did commercials, appeared in magazines, and even did box signings. Yes, he would show up in shopping malls and sporting events and sign boxes of cereal for screaming ten-year-old girls who were suddenly in love with a sugary breakfast food. He even got to be the judge for a competitive eating competition. His celebrity was kind of weird. I mean how could anyone become famous for smiling on a box of cereal? But at least it helped me keep track of him.

I didn't know why I needed to see his face all the time, but it could have been the fact that my life was falling apart in every other aspect. I wanted a piece of my old life. I wanted my life to be like it was when I lived in River's Bend and I couldn't shoot fire out of my fingers, I didn't have to chase evil villains to the ends of the Earth and my biggest worry was making sure the twins hadn't wiped snot on my dinner fork.

I talked with Tai and Elizabeth sometimes, but it wasn't enough. Tai was too far away and Elizabeth was busy most of the time. I just wanted someone to wrap their arms around me and say 'It's gonna be okay.' And I wanted that someone to be Kyle.

After visiting the Mini Frosted Funnel Cakes website for the fifth time in two hours, I learned that Kyle would be doing a box signing at Kansas City Royals game. I was going to be at that game. I had to see him.

"Priss, turn off the computer and meet us at the breakfast table," my dad said, poking his head in the family room. He had his cranky voice on. It wasn't his old cheery voice that used to get excited about a new cranberry orange muffin recipe he'd found. It was the cranky voice that I had gotten used to over the past month whenever he was near my mother.

I sat down at the table across from Josh. The twins sat next to him and my mom and dad were on opposite ends of the table. I couldn't help but notice how I was all alone on my side of the table.

"Kids, your dad and I have been talking and we both think it's best if we have some time apart."

Josh and I stared at each other with eyes wide.

"What do you mean time apart?" I asked in a panic.

"Do you mean divorce?" Josh asked.

"Oh my God, you're getting a divorce!" I said.

"Calm down, Priss," my dad said. "We didn't say divorce. We're just going to spend some time apart and think about things."

"It's more like a ... temporary separation," my mother added.

Josh and I stared at the table. The twins looked back and forth between my mom and dad. They weren't completely sure what was going on, but I think they were perceptive enough to know that something was wrong.

"How are you going to separate when you live in the same house?" Charlie asked.

"Yeah, won't you see each other all the time?" Chester added.

"We're not going to live in the same house, boys," my dad said.

Silence.

"So what does this mean for us?" I asked after what felt like ten minutes, but was probably more like ten seconds.

"Well, that's why we called this meeting," my mother said. "We all need to make some decisions."

I looked back and forth between my parents again. "Oh my God. You mean you want us to choose, don't you? Choose between you and Dad ... Right now?"

"It's not really that you have to choose, Priss," my dad said, trying to soften what felt like claws ripping my heart open. "I think we're going to eventually work it out so that you spend equal time with both of us. But, officially, one of us needs to be your primary guardian."

"And if you want to sleep on it and let us know in the morning, that will be fine," my mother added.

"Oh thanks, Mom. How generous of you to give us eight hours to decide the rest of our lives." I crossed my arms and slouched in my chair. I felt like my parents were tag teaming us in this attack on our lives.

"Oh don't be so dramatic, Priscilla. You'll still see your siblings and your estranged parent regularly. We'll still be a family, just in different houses." My mother tried to sound like her normal, calm, cool, collected self. I rarely saw my mother get emotional or lose control. But I knew this had to be killing her inside.

The kitchen was silent. How could they do this to us? How could they expect us to choose between them and at a moment's notice? It was completely unfair. I knew Josh had to agree with me. This was completely unacceptable and I was going to give them a piece of my mind.

"I choose Dad," Josh said out of the blue. I glared at him. How could he give in to this pressure? Maybe if we stuck together we could force them to change their mind. But no, he was just giving in after like two minutes. Once again, he was being selfish. I hated him even more.

"Very, well," my mother said, hiding the hurt in her voice. I looked over at my dad. If he was happy about winning Josh's affection he didn't show it. He just stared at his hands folded in front of him. "What about you Priscilla?"

"I ... I ... I... " I didn't quite know what I was going to say, but thankfully I was interrupted by the twins.

"We choose Dad, too," Chester said.

"Yeah, we want to live with Daddy," Charlie added.

My mother couldn't hide the tears welling in her eyes. She turned away and pressed her eyelids shut. Although we'd explained to them dozens of times that it wasn't really our mother that tried to kill Dad, that Selliwood was controlling her, I think they were still a little afraid of my mom deep down inside.

"If you want to live with your father as well, Prissy, I understand," she said not looking at me, but staring at the refrigerator as if it was going to help her or give her strength in some way.

What was I supposed to do in this situation? Of course, I loved my dad. And, honestly, I'd probably feel more comfortable living with him. He was the one who had taken care of me for the past three years while my mother battled Colonel Selliwood and his specimens. He may have been a little overprotective and wacky sometimes, but he was my dad and I loved him. But I loved my mom, too. And Charlie and Chester and Josh had abandoned her. I couldn't leave her alone. And I didn't even know if I could continue to live in the same house with Josh.

"No, Mom. I choose you. I want to live with you."

She looked at me as a tear spilled down her cheek. "You do?"

I nodded.

That night my mom and I met in my bedroom and made plans on where we would go and what we would do.

"This could be a great adventure for us, Prissy. What do you say we just buy a recreational vehicle and travel the country for a few months? Wouldn't that be fun?"

"But why do we have to leave?"

"Your Dad and I want to spend some time apart like we explained. Since he and your brothers are going to run the farm, we have to go somewhere else."

I shook my head. "Well, I don't want to live in an RV."

"Well, tell me what you want. We'll go anywhere you want. We can even live next to Disney World or something. Is that what you want?"

"No Mom, I want to go home. I want to go to River's Bend."

Thankfully, she understood my desire to go back to Pennsylvania. She hugged me and said, "Okay, we'll move back to River's Bend."

My mother also understood my need to go to that Kansas City Royals game and see Kyle. She took me herself.

***

Kyle, also known as the Mini Frosted Funnel Cakes kid, signed autographs until the first pitch was thrown out. Then he and his agent packed up and headed to the Mini Frosted Funnel Cakes van (which, by the way, was shaped like a giant funnel). I just skipped the autograph thing and waited by the van, the funnel shaped van. Really, who thinks of these things? Well, I guess it was better than driving around in a giant wiener like the Oscar Meyer people.

"No more autographs, kid," his agent said when he saw me.

"No, it's okay, Morris. I ... I know her," Kyle said, staring into my eyes as if he was looking at a ghost.

Morris shrugged and went into the van.

"What are you doing here, Priss?"

This is what I was afraid of. He didn't want to see me. What was I thinking? He probably hated me. The last time he saw me, I was kissing another boy.

"I ... I ... I ... " I couldn't think of anything to say so I just ran to him and wrapped my arms around him. Tears that I'd been holding in for a month started racing out of me with uncontrollable speed. Thankfully, he didn't push me away. He wrapped his arms around me and hugged me close as I soaked his shirt.

Given the fact that I don't think Kyle had ever seen me cry in my life, I was sure he was probably a little freaked out. I mean, I didn't even cry in the fourth grade when I broke my arm during a game of one on one basketball with him. I actually made him finish the game against me. When our parents showed up, they thought Kyle was the injured one since he was more upset than I was.

"Don't cry, Priss. It's going to be okay," he said, burying his face in my hair.

"Oh, Kyle. I've missed you so much. My life ... I can't ... "

"Just let it out, okay? I'm here for you." How could he be so understanding? The way he was just willing to wrap his arms around me without asking questions made me cry even more.

We sat down on the ground. Kyle leaned back against the van's front tire and continued to hold me against his chest. He stroked my hair while I breathed in his scent. Cherry lollipops mixed with his dad's Old Spice. It brought back so many memories.

When I had finally cried everything out of me, I leaned up and looked at him.

He wiped the tears off my cheeks with his fingertips and stared at me with his sweet blue eyes.

"Are you ready to tell me what's going on?" he asked.

I nodded. "There's so much I have to tell you, Kyle. It's time you knew everything."

Books by Sybil Nelson

Priscilla the Great

Priscilla the Great: The Kiss of Life

Priscilla the Great: Too Little Too Late

Priscilla the Great: Bring the Pain (February 2012)

Twin Shorts

And now for a sample from Twin Shorts!

Belly Boob Billy
Extra credit assignment (rough draft)

I used to love group work. I mean, my best friend Tai is a genius! Anytime we worked together in class, I was guaranteed an easy A. But, unfortunately, Tai is so smart that they put her in eighth grade this year, so bye-bye my one way ticket to automatic A-ville. As soon as the seventh grade science teacher Mr. Barkley (or Mr. Broccoli as everyone calls him) said we had a group project due on Friday, I died a little inside because I knew I would actually have to do work and with me and my lack of book skills, I knew an A was out of the question.

But it gets worse.

I was assigned to work with Billy Wescott. The infamous Billy Wescott. Kill me.

See Billy has an outie belly button which I hate. I know that seems petty, just wait, there's more. Normally the direction which someone's belly button poked wouldn't be a problem. But in Billy's case it was a huge issue. Billy liked to wear really tight shirts for some reason. Well, maybe he didn't really like it and was just forced into it because he had to wear hand me downs from his three older brothers. The older Wescott boys were skinny as string beans on SlimFast. I mean Coach Taylor forced Jamie Wescott to drink weight gain drinks for a month before he let him come near the high school football field.

Unfortunately, Billy didn't inherit the skinny gene. He was plump all over. So the clothing from his older brothers were a bit snug. That combined with his outie belly button made for some awkward situations.

When I talk to Billy Wescott it takes all of my

energy to make sure I focus on his face and not the nub sticking out of his stomach. How was I supposed to work with him alone for a week and overcome the temptation to stare?

Just to give you an idea of how bad the belly button situation is, once in fifth grade, Manny took a picture of Billy's belly cropped it just right, then sold copies of it for a dollar a piece. When the boys who bought the picture later figured out they weren't actually staring at a woman's breast, most of them were too embarrassed to ask Manny for their money back. Manny made a killing. That's also when poor Billy got the nickname Belly Boob Billy. Two years later, he was still saddled with the embarrassing name.

Enter my evil, annoying yet still pretty brilliant little brothers.

Billy and I were standing in my backyard working on our kinetic energy machine. Don't be impressed. We made a ramp out of cardboard then rolled my little brother's toy cars down it. Bam! Kinetic energy.

"Wow! It's huge!" Charlie said.

"I told you," Chester said.

I turned around to see what they were talking about and immediately got embarrassed.

"Boys, it's not polite to stare," I said pulling them away from where they were pointing at Billy's belly.

"It's okay," Billy said with a sigh. "Everyone does it."

"Are you sure?" I asked.

Billy nodded and then lifted up his shirt much to the delight of my little brothers who squealed and started dancing around Billy.

I put my head in my hands. I felt so bad for him. Was he doomed to go through life feeling like a circus freak?

My brothers pointed and stared at Billy's Belly for what felt like forever. Finally, Charlie looked at Chester and said, "Got it?"

Chester nodded and said, "Yep, got it."

I had no idea what they were talking about. I was just happy that they both turned and ran back into the house.

"I am so sorry about that, Billy."

He shrugged. "I don't even really care anymore," he said. But I could tell he did. His plump little face frowned as we went back to inspecting our machine. As if our cardboard ramp needed any further inspection. It was doomed for C-ville at best no matter what we named it.

Fifteen minutes later, Billy and I sat at my kitchen table sipping lemonade. All we could hear was the clanking of our ice cubes as I tried to think of something to say that would make him feel better about his deformity.

"I got a nasty hang nail on my big toe. Wanna see?" I asked excitedly as I slapped my foot on the table.

"Nah, that's okay. I better get home." Billy stood up and started heading for the door. Suddenly, my brothers burst into the kitchen so fast they nearly knocked him over.

"We got it!" Charlie and Chester said in unison while holding up an odd little contraption. It looked like it was part pantyhose, part socks, and part belt with some rubber bands weaved around it.

"Got what?" I asked.

"Here. It's for Billy," Charlie said waving in front of Billy's face.

"We think it will solve his belly boob problem," Chester added.

"What is it? Where did you get it from?" Billy asked. I could tell he was curious. Anything that might possibly end his days as the belly boob boy had to capture his attention.

"We made it," Chester said. "After studying your belly, we knew exactly what to do."

"Hey! Are those my pantyhose?" I yelled. "I told you brats to stay out of my room!"

"Here. Put it on," Charlie said ignoring me.

Billy looked at me as if asking if it was okay. I rolled my eyes and shrugged. Billy actually smiled as he took the contraption and headed to the bathroom to try it on.

About a minute later I was shocked by the new Billy. Not only did his belly button no longer stick out, but he looked like ten pounds thinner. My little brothers had essentially created a girdle with belly button hiding capabilities. It was amazing! I didn't know whether I was more shocked that it worked or that my brothers had created it.

There was so much potential for this little invention. I mean who knew how many other hundreds of kids out there suffered from the same thing as Billy? The twins could name their contraption and sell it on Ebay. I started to see some dollar signs in my mind. But first, this belly button thingie was gonna get me right on the train to A-ville!

12060697R10151

Made in the USA
Charleston, SC
09 April 2012